4/04

Custer, Terry, and Me

Other Five Star Titles
by G. G. Boyer:

Winchester Affidavit

Custer, Terry, and Me

A Western Story

G. G. BOYER

Five Star • Waterville, Maine

First Edition
First Printing: January 2004

Published in 2004 in conjunction with
Golden West Literary Agency.

Set in 11 pt. Plantin by Al Chase.

Printed in the United States on permanent paper.

Library of Congress Cataloging-in-Publication Data

Boyer, Glenn G.
    Custer, Terry, and me : a western story / by G.G. Boyer.
      p. cm.
    ISBN 1-59414-031-6 (hc : alk. paper)
    1. Custer, George Armstrong, 1839–1876—Fiction.
  2. Little Bighorn, Battle of the, Mont., 1876—Fiction.
  3. Dakota Indians—Wars, 1876—Fiction.   4. Generals—Fiction.   I. Title.
  PS3552.O8926C87 2004
  813'.54—dc22   2003061830

DEDICATION

The day I finished this book my brother
Donald R. Boyer,
age 83, not really old by today's standards, robbed of
a few more golden years by ill health
that stemmed from a lifetime of hard work,
died in Morris, Illinois.

Don was the model for Good Sam.
When others were in trouble,
he came running.

As my older brother,
whenever I needed him, he came running,
rescuing me from school yard bullies
and often from myself.

As Depression kids,
we were babes in the woods together,
and his lifelong example, as a human trait through the ages,
gave rise to that most cherished testimonial:

"I LOVED HIM LIKE A BROTHER."

Prologue

1945

This is my story.

It may impress some as unbelievable since no one has ever heard of me in the Custer myth. I will tell the full tale of how I got involved and how I found out what I think is the key to the disaster at the Little Big Horn, the event that General Alfred Terry dubbed a "sad and terrible blunder." In a lifetime of associating with other survivors, both white and red, I think I've put it all together. I had some incredible help, as I'll tell you.

It was June 28th, 1926. You may wonder what I was doing circling the Custer battlefield in an old World War I Jennie fifty years after Custer and five companies of his cavalry died there.

I had been trying to make it to the 50th anniversary memorial ceremonies, but got delayed. That was a big disappointment, since I wanted to gab with some of the old-timers I knew, but I had another more important reason. Anyhow, our Jennie broke down in Denver and we couldn't get parts in time to fix it and make it to the ceremonies.

I went up anyhow because of that more important reason: to keep a promise I'd made to someone to whom I owed a lot.

We circled high at first so I could see the whole route of the 7th Cavalry, from where I'd ridden with it across the

---

ridge from Rosebud Creek to the east into the Little Big Horn watershed. Fifty years earlier, we had uncertainly threaded down into the valley, knowing roughly where the Sioux and Cheyenne camps were because our Indian scouts had spotted them early that morning. None of the officers, including Custer, had been ready to believe the Indians were there in the vast numbers the scouts had estimated, although at least one officer later claimed he had. He told a lot of other lies, too, as I well know and will tell about.

If Custer had been certain of the numbers we were actually faced with, I'm sure he wouldn't have had the regiment advance in three separate battalions, since he had done that mainly to find out for sure about those numbers. From the advantage of hindsight, I wonder how little any of our officers with reputations as Indian fighters really knew about their tough adversaries. In addition to being ignorant, they weren't willing to believe their Indian scouts, who did know.

So we had been advancing in three battalions that had been formed for the dual purpose of a reconnaissance in force as well as to prevent the escape of the Indians. This is funny now to anyone who knows how we made out. But bear in mind that at the time no Army officer could conceive of the vast number of Indians actually there, and an Indian escape attempt was a reasonable assumption. It was what they always did, wasn't it?

As I said, the scouts had known where the Indian villages were and they had told Custer the location, but neither he nor his officers had quite believed them. The scouts had tried to show Custer from a high vantage point, but he had claimed to be unable to see what they did. Maybe his vision was beginning to fail him and he needed glasses. Who can say now?

These were the reasons why Captain Frederick Benteen with three companies had been sent off to the south to hit the Little Big Horn River, several miles upstream from where the final conflict occurred. There had been no fear that three companies of the 7th couldn't handle any number of Indians they were apt to encounter. In fact, Benteen's orders had been to "pitch into" anything he ran across. How ridiculous such an order was in the light of fact.

Custer with a battalion of five companies, and Major Marcus Reno with three, had advanced together down what is known today as Reno Creek, headed toward the suspected location of the main villages. I was with Custer and at his side a lot of the time because he looked out for me like I was his own kid. Shortly after Benteen's departure, we came to the place where a small outlying village had been. The Indians who had been there had left in a panic, no doubt caused by our approach, and had set fire to whatever they couldn't carry off. A teepee, with dead bodies inside, was still burning, which certainly testified to their surprise and haste. These dead had probably been killed a few days before in a fight with General George Crook that we didn't yet know about. Pity we hadn't known his fate. The whole campaign had been like an encounter in which a clumsy, blindfolded man was trying to grapple with a nimbler one not similarly handicapped. It had been a fool's errand considering the skimpy number of troops that had been assigned to the job from the first.

As I said before and want to emphasize, General Terry later dubbed it "a sad and terrible blunder." Who could have known better? But I wonder which blunder he meant? U.S. Grant's? William Sherman's? Phil Sheridan's? Terry's own, which was the worst of all?

I had seen the whole showdown coming on for a couple of

years because fate introduced me—a very unlikely candidate to have rubbed elbows with the mighty—to the principal actors. I know a lot that *isn't* in books. That's why I'm writing this.

I could see from our Jennie the whole panorama and could spot where the route and positions of various battalions had been. I knew where to look from maps I'd seen later and also from what I'd been told by others, since my own experience had been limited to what I'd observed with Custer's battalion.

The point of my story is about how and why these dispersed battalions ended up as they did, and how I was a part of it. The major tragedy took place on a ridge where the survivors of the five companies in Custer's battalion had been wiped out.

I asked my pilot—a war vet and barnstormer—to circle low over the long bluff that's called Last Stand Hill today. I could have ended up there myself except that one of the last things Custer had done was send me off with a message—probably to get me out of harm's way, since I was still just a kid. If I'd stayed with him, I wouldn't be telling this story. Custer had given me my orders at the foot of a large ravine called Medicine Tail Coulée. There was a ford there on the Little Big Horn.

The firing hadn't started there until just after I left. We had heard firing from Reno's battalion for at least twenty minutes before that. After I left on Custer's order, I cut up a ridge at an angle. The firing from behind prompted me to stop and look back. What I saw caused me to dig in spurs and pull my freight in a helluva panic. Some Indians had already infiltrated between my position and the action at the ford. They ignored me, but in any case I was on a very fast horse and they probably couldn't have caught me. Even at that my chances to escape hadn't been red hot, except that I had joined two of the Crow scouts who were also headed to hell out of trouble as fast as their horses could carry them. The lifelong fighting experience of those two, White Man Runs Him and Hairy Moccasin, saved my bacon. I'd probably have tried to rejoin one of the battalions and blundered into more hostiles. The two Crows, veterans of many Indian fights, knew when it was a time to fight and a time to run. They had been running. If it had been up to them, the whole outfit would have run early that morning and taken up a defensive position, most likely somewhere along the mouth of Reno Creek where there was plenty of water in easy reach that could have been held by the whole regiment.

If I had had any ideas about not deserting my friends, these two scouts changed them. I could get by in Crow lingo pretty well by then. The sum of what they had told me was that everyone down there was going to be wiped out. It sure had looked that way to me. As a street kid I'd learned to think for myself. I decided to stick with the two Crow scouts.

Looking down from our circling plane at the rough jumble of ridges and gullies, I tried to pick out the escape route we three had followed. We had been able to cut between the five doomed companies of Custer's battalion and the Indians coming from Reno's disastrous repulse to join the fight against Custer. There was a ridge to the east with timber on it, and we had headed for it. We knew that if we made it there, we could abandon our horses, if need be, and hide in the rocks.

I was back a half century. Even after so much time had passed, my heart was pounding and I felt again the oppressive taste of deep fear, the way you feel when you know you have a pretty good chance of being killed and wonder what dying feels like.

Afternoon, June 25, 1876

We three pulled in our horses for a short breather and looked back to see if any Sioux were after us. We were well east of the Last Stand fight by then, on our way to timber. All we could make out was the distant smoke and dust of the fighting on Last Stand Hill. We found a gully that led to the crest of a hill and hid there. We could also see Reno's and Benteen's forces assembled, and we wondered why they didn't move to the sound of the fighting. There was nothing to prevent them from doing it for at least two hours. Finally the diminishing volume of cavalry carbine fire carried an unmistakable message to us to get farther away, right quick.

Hairy Moccasin said to me: "Come with us. We have to get away if we can."

We swung northeast, first at a fast trot on the rough ground, then at a high lope as soon as we could. It was obvious that Custer's plans had come unglued and the whole regiment might be blown to glory by sundown.

General Terry had assigned the Crow scout detachment to Custer, under the leadership of Mitch Boyer. Just after Custer rode down Medicine Tail Coulée to the ford on the Little Big Horn, he had sent the two Crow scouts to see if they could get a sight of Reno's retreating column. I'll tell you later why he expected Reno to be retreating.

I decided to accept the invitation of my Crow friends to ride back to their reservation with them. They'd got their bellies full of white man tactics, and so had I. I was sickened by what I'd seen, and tired of civilization. Besides, I knew Custer, one of the best friends I'd ever had, was dead. Like Huck Finn, after seeing a buddy killed in a feud, I wanted to forget the whole thing and go back to a freer life.

★ ★ ★ ★ ★

By the time I came back, it was too late to tell what I knew. It blew sky-high the stories that had been concocted to clear various skirts. No one would believe me anyhow. They had refused to believe the Indians who told the same story. In my case, I couldn't be sure that telling what I knew wouldn't have put my life in danger. As I discovered in time, it certainly would have. Lots of people kill to maintain a reputation, and Army officers are no exception—and, if we face the facts, they actually provide some of the major examples of the type. I learned that almost to my sorrow. The Indians shortly learned it, too, and kept their stories to themselves. Many of the Sioux and Cheyennes were even afraid to come to the 50th anniversary memorial ceremony for fear the whites were luring them there to kill them at last, for revenge. How sad.

Chapter One

The main reason I learned the inside story about the big Sioux war of 1876 was because I had got run over by the buggy in which Captain R. P. Hughes was driving General Terry to headquarters one morning in the spring of 1873. Hughes was Terry's brother-in-law and aide. They must have been running late and were clipping right along. The headquarters of the Army's Department of Dakota was in St. Paul, at the corner of 4th and Wabashaw.

Like a kid, I was trying to run across the road before they got there, and for no good reason. I slipped in the muddy slush of melting snow from a late blizzard and got run down by the team. It knocked the wind out of me and I got a big lump on my head. I don't remember much about it, so I must have been knocked out. When I came around, the general himself was holding me up in a sitting position and trying to pump some breath back into me. He didn't know much about medicine or he'd have known that, if I had some broken ribs, he might have killed me. Anyway, the first thing I remember was this big, bearded man—the general—holding me, and he looked really concerned, like he might cry if I died.

The way I felt I wasn't sure I might not die, and I remember thinking: *This is funny. I never expected to get killed when I woke up this morning.*

In a little while a cop trotted up, and then a pretty good crowd collected since we were right downtown when it happened. None of them really seemed to know what to do. I—heard a woman saying—"The poor thing."—but she didn't offer to baby me like some would have.

A man ran up, carrying a satchel, and said: "I'm a doctor, let me look at the kid. Get back and give him some air."

The general must have figured that didn't apply to him because he stayed right beside me.

After the doc felt me over and asked a few questions about where I hurt, he said: "I guess you're mostly just shook up. Where's your home? We'll get you there and put you to bed and have your ma look after you."

That's where I got drafted into the Army, you might say. I just said the plain truth, which was: "I ain't got a home."

I can still hear the general's voice right now as plain as the day he said it. "No home?" Kinda a rising note in it, like he'd never heard of anyone who didn't have a home and couldn't believe it—at least not about a kid my age, which was about fourteen. He wasn't aware of the gritty real world around him—there must have been a dozen like me in St. Paul. It wasn't too bad in summer, but winters were tough.

Anyhow, when he asked me about not having a home, all I said was: "No, sir." There wasn't much else to say. I wanted to run, especially with a cop there, but I was still too shook up. Street kids like me learned to avoid cops if we could.

A lot of people were standing around, listening, and even the doctor stayed to hear my story although he was sure by then that I wasn't hurt bad.

"Where do you live if you haven't got a home?" the general asked.

"Around. Mostly down by the river."

The general turned to Captain Hughes and said: "We're going to take this boy out to the fort for now. I want to help him if we can."

He looked around to see if anyone had any objections, not that he'd have paid any attention. Everyone in St. Paul knew that General Terry was a big stick in the community and that he and his family were into all the local charities and uplift societies. Besides, the fort—Fort Snelling—was good for business.

That's how come I rode out to Fort Snelling with General Terry. He and the captain took me around to one of the companies there and saw that I got a good meal thrown into me, and that impressed me more than anything else. I hadn't had a square meal in so long I couldn't remember. I'd worked at odd jobs but never earned enough to eat on regularly, or pay for a place to stay. My kind panhandled the restaurants or went through the garbage out back when no one was looking.

I know now it caused quite a stir in that mess hall when the general brought in a ragamuffin kid and sat down at the same table with him, but at the time I didn't think anything of it. Captain Hughes was right along with him and the mess sergeant hung around and waited on us hand and foot, which you'd expect if you know anything about the Army. I didn't know that officers didn't usually eat in the same place as the men.

The general said: "I'll just have a cup of coffee, if you don't mind, Sergeant. How about you, Hughes?"

The sergeant said: "Yes, sir, General, and I'd be glad to fix something special for the general if he wants."

"Coffee will be fine," Terry said.

That was the first time I ever heard the Army custom of referring to high-ranking officers in the third person, like "the general this" and "would the general that?" Sort of like talking to God, you might say. And, believe me, generals were treated like gods in those days. It was a helluva good job.

After I ate, the general and Hughes drove me over to a Sergeant Clery's office. He was the sergeant major, which is the chief administrative non-commissioned officer on a fort.

"He's been shook up pretty bad, Clery," the general told him. "Keep an eye on him for a few days, and find some light work for him when he's able to get around. He can be some company's mascot or something for a while. But I feel responsible for him, so, if there's any expense, I'll foot the bill. We ran over him in the buggy, and we owe him. I'll be out to check every few days, and, if he's hurt worse than the doctor thought, get him into the hospital right away and get a doctor on the case and let me know immediately."

He didn't have to tell Clery to tell the doctor he would be speaking for the commanding general because everyone on the post knew Clery did that.

Young and green as I was, I could tell that Clery and the general were more than just a sergeant and an officer by the tone of voice in which Clery said: "Yes, General. I'll see to it."

Later I found out Clery and the general had been through the war together and they were more like friends than a non-com and a general. Clery was the sort that the general liked to keep around him—a clean-cut fellow of the kind that always reminded me of schoolteachers who looked younger than they must have been. Hughes was the same sort—sort of effeminate you'd say today.

Custer kept his inner circle, too, but they weren't the same sort. John Burkman, for example, who was his orderly, was really a diamond in the rough, but sure wasn't a schoolteacher type. He was from old Southern feuding stock. In the next couple of years I got to know Custer almost as well as I did Terry.

I didn't know, when I was sprawled out there on my back in the spring slush and mud of a St. Paul street, that I was going to end up about like Huck Finn, getting civilized and rubbing elbows with history. Fort Snelling was the start of it, and it was sure an eye-opener.

Until Terry found me, I'd only seen the fort on its hill from a distance. Kids like me stayed away from the Army just like we tried to stay away from the cops. Soldiers and cops both wore uniforms and represented law and order, so we figured they might do something to us since we couldn't be very law abiding or orderly under their rules—not and manage to survive. Maybe that early need to skirt authority gave me a clearer insight into the Indians' problems when I met a lot of them later.

The thing I liked best at the fort was the mess hall. I was impressed, like any kid would be, by cannons sitting around here and there, but you can't eat cannons.

Because I came into that mess hall the first time with the general, the mess sergeant buttered me up and invited me in when I was passing by one day later on. After that, I could drop in anytime and be fed. I must have gained ten pounds the first month I was out at the fort.

Clery put me to work in the stables and around the grounds. I loved horses and the outdoors. He kept a fatherly eye on me and came around almost every day and clapped his arm around my shoulders like a father and had something to say about how I was doing. I figured he probably wanted kids of his own but had never married, like so many of those old Army professionals.

I slept in a company barracks with the troops. It was really nice to have my own mattress and blankets and be warm at night. There was a big stove in the center of the barracks and a soldier was detailed as night guard to keep it going. A different soldier pulled that duty for a week at a time and got out of all other duties, even drill, and could sleep all day if he wanted to. Naturally almost all of them liked duty as night guard.

They decked me out with Army clothes, too, though I looked kind of like a scarecrow, I guess, until I filled out a little. I liked them anyhow, since they were warm and didn't have any holes in them to let in cold air, whether they looked fancy or not.

Nobody picked on me at first, though you'd expect someone coming along, like I did, would be seen as a teacher's pet. Sergeant Clery probably saw to that. But sooner or later someone was bound to try hazing me, thinking they could be sneaky and get away with it. That was the Army of it. We had some real low types, but not many. In those days everyone decent was raised knowing they were supposed to take care of little guys, and feed stray dogs and cats, and that sort of thing. Even most of the rough class that made a career of the Army had that pounded into their characters young. It was the American way then, and I hope it always will be.

That's how I met Paddy O'Toole. He was a new recruit, but anyone could tell he'd been a soldier somewhere. He was just a private and had the bunk next to mine. I had the end bunk in the row right next to the non-coms' room where a corporal and sergeant lived. There was a door there that led directly outside.

Someone took the notion that I ought to be indoctrinated like most recruits were, especially since I was Clery's and the general's pet, as they naturally saw it. The first I learned about it was when I was startled out of a sound sleep by having my bunk tipped over in the dark. I landed with a thump, dazed and wondering what had happened, and it didn't feel good, either, since I hit my head pretty hard on the floor. Whoever did it bolted out the door and ran like hell. Naturally it woke up everyone in the barracks. Someone lit a lamp. There was a general laugh, but Paddy O'Toole didn't laugh, just wanted to know if I was hurt.

In the old Army they called that bunk dumping business "barreling". It happened to a lot of recruits and was all part of the game.

Paddy patted my shoulder and helped me get my bed back together, and we all turned in again. He said: "Forget it, kid. It's all part of getting to know the boys. Probably had a drink or two in him, whoever did it."

Up till then Paddy had hardly so much as said a word to me. Come to think of it, he'd said very little to anyone else, either. He was the kind that kept to himself and wasn't much for talking. No one took offense over it, either. The word was he'd been a boxer and had given some of the best of them a run for their money. Someone had also heard that Paddy might be dodging the law, but a lot of soldiers were.

A couple of nights went by and I had trouble getting to sleep for fear someone might barrel my bunk again, then I forgot about it. That's when it happened the second time, and again the next night. The following evening I was almost scared to go to bed, but I didn't have anywhere else to sleep and was always pretty tired after a day's work. A lot of the men were sympathetic and word got to Sergeant Clery. He probably would have moved me out of there, but, as it turned out, he didn't have to. Paddy lay awake that night, waiting for whoever the bully was, and, like a fool, the joker pushed his luck too far. The fuss woke up everyone, with a voice yelling like they were being killed. Lamps were soon lit all over the barracks, and Sergeant Morgan, who had the room in our barracks, came out and said: "What the hell is going on here?"

What was going on was that Paddy had a man in a hammer lock and was almost breaking his arm. The fellow he'd grabbed wasn't a midget, either. Paddy was broad and beefy and must have stood five foot ten, but whoever it was stood half a head taller. But Paddy was a pro and a match for him. He turned him around, and the fellow tried to put up his dukes, but Paddy hit him in the stomach and doubled him up, then decked him with a roundhouse to the side of his head, and he fell like a tree and shook the floor when he hit it.

"You mean son-of-a-bitch!" Paddy growled, looking down at him. "Anyone know him?"

It turned out he was from the next barracks, a private named Smith—yeah, that's a laugh—there were a lot of Smiths, also Joneses, in the Army. We never figured out why he'd decided to pick on me because he wasn't around long enough after that.

After someone threw a bucket of water on him, he sat up and, even before he got on his feet, asked: "What son-of-a-bitch hit me? I wasn't ready. I'll get even for that."

Paddy said: "I'm the son-of-a-bitch you're looking for. And no son-of-a-bitch like you gets away with calling me his brother."

Sergeant Morgan never said a word or did a thing to put a stop to it. That wasn't the old Army way. In fact, he went back into his room. He knew there'd be a staged match after supper the next day, out behind the stables. That's the way those things were taken care of. There was a set-to almost every week, and usually whoever lost shook hands with the winner and that was the end of it. But Smith wasn't that kind.

The next day everyone not on duty turned out to watch the fight, and I was there with them. I even spotted Sergeant Clery back in the crowd, not wanting to be too obvious since no one officially recognized this sort of law and order, and he might have been expected to stop it ahead of time in the event someone really got hurt.

Smith had to get off some blow. He yelled: "You'll have to fight me this time fair and square, you little bastard! I guess you're sweet on the kid!"

Everyone knew what he meant, and Paddy got red in the face, but didn't say anything except: "Don't talk so much."

Smith came on like a barroom brawler, all muscle but no science, and Paddy let him get in a couple of roundhouse swings that he ducked. Then he did a repeat of the night before and chopped Smith down, but he didn't hit him hard enough to put him away. He wanted to hurt him some more. Smith got up groggy, blood on his face from his cut lip. He shook his head to clear it, then rushed in blindly and tried to grapple with Paddy who spun him around, then danced behind him, waiting. Smith rushed again and took a couple of quick, hard chops to the face that started him bleeding even more, from both the nose and mouth, though it didn't take the fight out of him.

By then the crowd had its blood up. Some of the men from Smith's outfit were cheering for him, not that they liked bullies, but a lot of them didn't know what the fight was about, and, even if they had, company rivalry was always a big thing. Smith was their man, right or wrong. They were in for a big disappointment. He never landed a punch on Paddy and got himself ground up into hamburger before Paddy dropped him with a punch that would have knocked down a bull. That was the end of it. It took ten minutes to bring him around.

Paddy said to me after he'd cleaned up and we were going to bed: "Stay out of his way. He might try to take it out on you."

The thought of that scared hell out of me. I could imagine him grabbing me in the dark some night. But, as it turned out, I had nothing to worry about. Smith was gone the next day and took with him a few of the personal possessions of the

22

men who had cheered him on. He may not have been afraid to get hurt some more, but the loss of face, aside from the way he'd lost a lot of it literally, was too much for one of his kind. He went "over the hill", which was soldier lingo for deserting.

Usually the first sergeant could whip anyone in the company, which was why he got the job. If he got whipped, they made the winner first sergeant if he wasn't too dumb to handle the paperwork, not that they couldn't get a clerk to handle that for him. It was a good system to see that the troops all did what the first sergeant, or "first soldier" as he was called, told them to.

Everyone figured it was only a matter of time before they made Paddy a first sergeant. He wasn't too dumb to handle paperwork, either. A few years later I gave him a job on the railroad that he held for thirty years. The main thing that pleased me at the time was that, at Fort Snelling, no one tried to pick on me again.

Actually Smith was lucky. If General Terry had heard about the affair, I'm sure the system would have found a way to put Smith where he'd be breaking up rocks with a sledge-hammer or, as they called it, "making little ones out of big ones" for a few years, behind the walls of some prison. Generals, as I said, were a little like gods in those days.

Chapter Two

It wasn't long before General Terry's sisters heard about me. As Mark Twain might have said: "That's when the trouble started."

My notion is that they all wanted kids of their own, but, like the general, except for Clara who married Captain Hughes, none of them married. Hughes ranked and drew pay as a captain—but as the general's aide, even if he did look sort of sissified, everyone knew he spoke for the general, so he might as well have worn a star.

Anyhow, the trouble started because the general's sisters all lived with him at one time or another, even Harriet, although I didn't meet her till years later, since she was a principal at Vassar College when I first became a member of the Terry tribe.

The general had a big, brick mansion in St. Paul, surrounded by trees and gardens. When the ladies heard about me from Hughes and the general, I was promoted out of the barracks to live with the Terrys. That was "to get me out of" what I later heard one of the girls call the "degrading influence" of the barracks. They gave me my own room upstairs in the carriage house, which was a lot better than a barracks for sure. They all came to see me, and I was occasionally invited to the big house. Even the general dropped in, now and again. He was like Clery, hugging me like I was the son he always wanted. Actually I've never been the type to like that sort of personal display of affection, probably because I had had such a tough row to hoe and never got that sort of warm treatment from my own family. I never told the general, however, even when I thought he overdid it a little. He wasn't the type that people wanted to hurt. Around his family he was sort of a big boy. They loved it, and I think a lot of others liked that side of him best, too.

Like every alleged blessing, his fondness for me had its penalties. Perhaps adopting his attitude, the Terry girls all thought I needed to be polished. I don't remember which of them cornered me first—probably Fanchon, which was what the family all called Fanny—about dancing, of all things. As I remember, it went about like this.

"How would you like to learn to dance?"

The fact of the matter was, it had never occurred to me, and I couldn't think of what to say. I confess I sort of wondered if she meant like the Indians did, since that was the only kind of dancing I knew about. Anyhow the question didn't look to me like it left me much to say, so I didn't say anything. She thought I was reluctant, rather than simply confused.

She said: "When you grow up and go out in society, you'll need to dance to associate with the right people."

I got a picture of the farmers in the coulée back in Wisconsin, who *were* the *right* kind of people the way I saw it, and wondered what difference dancing would have made to them. Most of them were too tired to dance after hoeing their row every day from sunup to sundown.

She sensed my problem and applied a little salesmanship. "The general is going to see to it that you go to the right schools from now on, and you'll move *up* in society. He even mentioned getting you an appointment to West Point if you study hard and can pass the examinations."

I said the first thing that came to mind and blurted out: "What is West Point?"

She looked stunned. Although General Terry wasn't a West Pointer, the U.S. Military Academy was a sacred institution in the Army then, and I guess it still is. Somehow I have never regarded it as a great tragedy that General Terry's plans for me along those lines never materialized.

She actually gasped, then recovered and smiled. "You've never heard of the U.S. Military Academy at West Point?"

"No, ma'am," I confessed.

"Then that shows that you should go there," she stated positively.

I'd never heard of the Vatican, either, but I'll wager that, if Fanny had found that out, she wouldn't have taken a notion to prepare me for a Jesuit seminary.

That's when my first real schooling started. St. Paul had pretty good public schools, and I didn't mind it for a while, since I always wanted to learn as much about everything as I could. The problem was that I learned so fast, it got boring to sit around and wait for the boobs to get something through their heads. That's when I started to moon out the school window at the distant woods and river and, shortly, started skipping school.

Naturally my truancy got reported to the Terrys. There were a lot of tearful sessions over my "backsliding" among the sisters, who all mourned for my wayward soul, especially Lilly, as I recall, and a few sessions with the general in which he not only mourned for my wayward soul, but gave me a pep talk about becoming a responsible citizen. Sad for me, I knew even then that his notion of a responsible citizen boiled down to a "dude", especially one of the types that wore evening clothes to the dinner table. I was lucky there. The whole family had sufficient caution that I was never at the dinner table, or treated to a suit of evening clothes. The best I did was eat at the second table in the kitchen with the servants. It beat not eating at all by a whole bunch. Maybe if I'd gone to West Point and graduated, I'd have been promoted to the first table.

They must have had some interesting discussions about sending me to dancing school—maybe they sent me to salve their consciences at not being *quite* democratic enough to accept me completely. I'd rather have been sent to a pool hall.

Imagine a street urchin who was prone to skip school being sent to dancing school every Thursday evening! The contortions we went through there went by the name of "cotillion", and I wondered what the hell that meant. At the time I never bothered to find out. I managed to get most of the boys there to start smoking or chewing. Luckily we were never found out. I can imagine my fate if we had been.

They got me a set of Little Lord Fauntleroy clothes to pirouette in. I wondered what my old chums down by the river would say if I wore those duds when I sneaked what food I could down to them. They might have drowned me in the drink if I had.

I guess I ought to mention my distinguished name, since I haven't so far. It's Tom Ballard.

Chapter Three

1945

We've had three wars since Custer was killed. The one we're in now is World War II. I've pulled through a long while, and it looks like I'll live through this one, too. That Wisconsin coulée farm and my life as a street kid like Huck Finn in St. Paul don't seem real any more. Here I am in what some people would call a mansion. On a clear day Ican look down across the swimming pool in the clipped and trimmed back yard and see the Pacific behind a row of manicured palm trees, tide thundering in and out below the cliffs, a view that stretches away until it evaporates into the horizon. I can't hear the surf any more, and miss that. Getting old and half deaf and needing glasses really doesn't show me a hell of a lot.

This place is a big old barn, too big for me alone, but I lived my happiest years here with my wife. I'm not about to sell it. I can afford servants to help me keep it up, especially Maggie, my maid, who thinks she's my mother even though I'm old enough to be her father. But for all of that, I'm really alone again. I know it bothers Maggie. She brings her grandkids up here, every once in a while, to brighten up the place. She doesn't ask and knows she doesn't have to. My ears are good enough to hear a noisy crowd of kids, and I sure love to hear them yelling and splashing in the swimming pool, or babbling out in the kitchen with Maggie, while they're raiding the refrigerator. They call me Uncle Tom. I wonder if they know who Uncle Tom was in history. Uncle Tom's tear-jerking rôle in the popular book, *Uncle Tom's Cabin*, practically started the Civil War, and Lincoln once told Tom's creator, Harriet Beecher Stowe, as much when he greeted her in a White House reception line.

At night here in this big barn, when everything is quiet, I have visitors I never mention to anyone. At my age, a lot of ghosts are apt to collect if you've lived the sort of life that attracts them. I've noticed that ghosts are generally those whose lives were cut short by a violent death. It seems that folks robbed of a full life don't want to leave without collecting the rest of their due. If the reader doesn't want to believe in spooks, I can't help it. I hear footsteps at night when I'm alone, and sometimes voices I recall from the past.

I can hear coyotes, too, with no trouble provided there's no other noise—but the coyotes are *live* critters, hunting the arroyos that run down to the ocean. I love their hair-raising yelping, a sound that brings back the wide, lonesome prairies of Dakota and Montana in the 1870s. Sometimes I hear trace chains of the long lines of wagons that always went with the Army on campaign, and the rumble that only thousands of horses' and mules' hoofs, beating the hard, sun-baked earth in rhythm, can make. I feel sad whenever I stop to think that all of those faithful animals, including my horse Buns, are dead now, and likely most of the people who managed them.

It has all sadly gone, and, like most old people, I remember the early days best, the friends of my youth. I was leading a really lonely life when Maggie decided to take a hand. It's a good thing for this story that she did, since it's given me some modern slang that I think makes my story easier to understand for today's readers, assuming I ever have any.

It started one warm afternoon when I was dozing off while trying to read in my big chair in the library and I noticed Maggie fussing around the vicinity longer than necessary. I knew she had something on her mind.

Finally she said: "Why don't *we* invite some of those lonesome soldiers up here on weekends? Most of 'em go out when they get their passes and spend what little money they have. They end up with not enough to eat on and some can't pay their fare to get back to wherever they're stationed, so they end up in trouble."

I thought: *Soldiers never change.* Then I wondered how Maggie knew so much about what soldiers did. She sure wasn't dating them at sixty or so, although she was still a pretty spry-looking chicken, considering.

It sounded good to me. I told her: "Hop to it. I always got along with soldiers just fine." I remembered that warm barracks back at Fort Snelling and Paddy O'Toole and the rest that I had known. It sounded like a good idea to me, so nowadays *we* invite a lot of lonely G.I.s out here when they get a pass, and I'm glad we do. Some of them have already fought their war and come home. Out here on the West Coast we have a lot of military bases.

I take a lot of the G.I.s who come up here out on the town to places they'd never be able to afford. They even get to rub elbows with the movie crowd every once in a while. You can be sure I never think I'm exposing them to a world they might otherwise never know in order to prepare them to get *up* in society like the Terry sisters did with me. I just want them to have a good time before they go out and maybe get killed. And I swear I've never tried to send a one to Arthur Murray's Dancing School so they'll fit into polite society if they survive the war. Most of them suit me just fine the way they are.

I thought a long while before tipping my hand and telling anyone that I'm the last of the Mohicans. That is, except for ghosts. I decided to jump to the present to tell my story and do it just like we're sitting here having a little talk. By jumping to 1945, you know I lived through it all. I want the truth to live after me, so I aim to take advantage of the human tendency to say—"He's probably right . . . after all, he was there, he knew them all."—especially about my opinions of characters in the Custer story. Also, knowing I'm still around, the reader will realize my opinions are based on a lot more than I knew from just being there at the time. By now I've read dozens of articles and books that have been written about it, some based on the stories of guys who lived through Custer's campaigns in the 1870s, like I did. I knew most of them—visited or corresponded with a lot of them until they passed away, one by one. I've had some of them visit here, too. It gave me a lot of food for thought. And telling a story after you've had time to think about it a good many years helps a writer make educated guesses about what this or that person must have been thinking at a key point.

The ghosts first came one night when I was dozing comfortably in my chair, here, in the library. They startled me, as you can imagine, and before I write it down, you should know that Custer's first name was George, and the family nickname for him was Autie, and his wife's name was Libbie. The voice I heard sounded like someone reading poetry.

"George!
Autie!
Are you listening?
You never suspected you weren't bulletproof did you?
There you lie, mute and white, with two bullet holes in you."

"Actually you were crazy as hell!
But magnificent!
You rode a big horse flat out, always in front in the Civil War,

31

swinging a long sword and yelling like the maniac you were. Christ, how your men worshipped you! And how Libbie worshipped you! She followed you almost to the battlefields where you fought."

"And remember Anthony Wayne? Of course, you remember Anthony Wayne . . . your pa's mean bull that everyone told you to stay away from. You never knew why. He always let you pet him on the nose, and you would say to him . . . 'Hey, bull, come with me and I'll pick you some grass from the other side of the fence.' And he would lumber along right behind you. You were all of three years old.

At West Point the shade of General Mad Anthony Wayne, who they named that bull for, was your counselor. He was your model of a general because he'd been President Washington's picked man, who'd kicked hell out of the Shawnees up in the country where you were born. Ran the British out finally, too . . . the damned Lobsterbacks who refused to get out even after they lost the Revolutionary War.

Good thing that you never told anyone at the Point that you talked to Mad Anthony Wayne. Really you couldn't have had a better oracle than old Mad Anthony, but they'd have carted you away to an asylum if you'd insisted he was real."

"Of course, Mad Anthony was real!
But was Mad Autie real?"

"What voice is that? Is that you, Mad Anthony? What's that? You hauled Autie straight to Valhalla? Well, say hello to Thor next time you're there. He and Autie should get along well."

"What did you say?
'Don't count on it?' "

"Come to think of it that makes sense."

Chapter Four

A fantastic dream? Probably. But it sounded so true about him that I woke up grinning. I remember when I first saw Custer in the flesh. What a sight! I can express my reaction by quoting someone who saw him just after he got his first star as a brigadier general in the Civil War. He thundered past, riding hell-for-leather to join his brigade, just before Gettysburg. The astonished observer said: "The son-of-a-bitch had more gold braid on his uniform than a French admiral and rode like a circus rider gone crazy. His staff was strung out a mile behind him, trying to keep up."

Well, I got to meet Autie by accident because General Terry thought I ought to amount to something. The general put me to work with Captain William Ludlow, his staff engineer. I started out as a rod and chainman, and gradually learned surveying, then practical engineering. That's how I got into railroading with Jim Hill, a few years later, and made the money that landed me here in this pile of fancy pink brick by the Pacific. But learning to dance at a cotillion never contributed a nickel's worth to my rise in the world.

In 1874, Ludlow was sent along as engineer on an Army exploration campaign to the Black Hills. Commander of the expedition was Custer, and the escort troops were naturally from his 7th Cavalry. There was a lot more to it than exploration, though, and it all led to Custer's Last Stand.

In any case we—Ludlow and a lot of his staff and some other officers from headquarters, with me along—took a Northern Pacific train to Bismarck, which was then the end of the line, and were ferried across the Missouri River to Fort Abraham Lincoln, since the railroad hadn't built a bridge across the Missouri yet.

I was riding with Ludlow when we pulled up in front of Custer's headquarters at Fort Lincoln in an Army ambulance that passed for a taxi in those days. We got there just as a rider thundered up, bareback, on a big bay horse. They skidded to a stop in front of headquarters, scattering dust and troopers and anything else in the way, and the rider nimbly jumped to the ground. A pack of greyhounds was running with him and buried him in a pooch pile as soon as he jumped off, all trying at once to jump on him and lick him to death.

Our horses almost ran away over the spectacle.

"That's Custer," Ludlow told me.

He didn't have to tell me. Circus rider gone crazy wasn't the half of it.

Dogs loved him as much as he loved them. And remember, if dogs love a fellow, he can't be all bad. Keep that in mind when you hear what Custer's enemies had to say about him. He had a lot of those, mostly due to jealousy, and foremost among them was Captain Fred Benteen.

West Pointers, especially classmates, had no rank between them when they were off duty, so Custer and Ludlow embraced like long-lost brothers, pounding each other on the back. I was startled when Ludlow called Custer Fanny and learned that Ludlow was Spike. Actually Ludlow was a freshman when Custer graduated, but they were at the Point together, which is almost the same as being classmates. In fact, Ludlow was the reason Custer graduated a little late, but that's another story.

When they got untangled, Custer looked me over and asked: "Who is this?"

"General Terry's ward," Ludlow said. "He works for me as a chainman and does a good job, too."

I almost fainted when Custer offered his hand just as though I were a grown man. I didn't know yet that he had the touch with youth—when he *wanted* to. Why shouldn't he have? He had led thousands of them during the Civil War and they had worshipped him. He was a boy himself to the day he died, and probably would have remained one if he'd lived to be a hundred. Custer was also no stranger to apple-polishing. I wonder now if Ludlow had deliberately put in the information that I was General Terry's ward. He knew that was stretching it a little, but he also knew it would get me a privileged position in the coming campaign. He liked me. I was a hard worker and learned fast.

Ludlow's choice of words saved me from billeting with the rest of his crew in the troop barracks. I got a room in the Custer quarters, shared with brother Tom Custer. To fit in extra guests, the Custers simply moved in Army cots to accommodate any number of bodies. Ludlow had his own private room. The place was big as a barn. Commanding officers did pretty well for living quarters even on the frontier.

The Custer quarters I lived in on my first visit burned down that winter and was replaced by an even fancier one. In case you wonder how a penny-pinching Army managed such things, Custer was the fair-haired boy of General Phil Sheridan, commander of the Army's Missouri Division. Sheridan was naturally the key figure in whacking up the budget when it filtered down to the field. Custer always did all right. A few years before, when he was superficially in official disgrace, sentenced by a court-martial to surrender his rank and pay for a year, General Sheridan had given him his own quarters to live in at Fort Leavenworth, if and when the Custers wished to use them. And, come to think of it, after Custer was long dead, his portrait was the only one on the wall of Sheridan's office when he became Commanding General of the Army, and I know that for sure because I saw it there myself.

I was just about to meet Custer's wife Libbie and, after I learned more, wondered if her picture didn't belong on Sheridan's office wall instead of the boy general's, not that there was any Bathsheba hanky-panky going on, but Sheridan was sweet on her. Almost every man that ever met her was. Sheridan had bought the table on which Grant and Lee had signed the surrender terms for Lee's army at Appomattox and sent it to her via her husband. It didn't hurt to have a wife who could further your Army career, and still doesn't.

After Custer turned over his horse Dandy to an orderly and ducked into his office and back out, he led the way with a rapid stride to his quarters, talking to Ludlow in his nervous, high-pitched voice.

"You probably know what we're really after with this reconnaissance," he said.

"Pretty much."

I didn't and was all ears.

"Sheridan plans to put a couple of forts over in the Black Hills. It isn't policy to mention it yet, but it's bound to happen. Sooner or later the Sioux have to go onto reservations, the poor devils. It will just about kill them. They're real men and want to roam free the way they always have. Who can blame them? But sooner or later this country will be full of ranches, and even farms and towns, and the old days will go. I'll hate that as bad as the Sioux." He laughed abruptly in what was almost a snort. "I suppose they'll put me on a reservation, too. Like Sturgis."

Sturgis, a full colonel to whom Custer, as a lieutenant colonel, was second in command, was the official commanding officer of the 7th Cavalry, but Sheridan knew how much good he'd be against Indians. He kept Sturgis on administrative duty, serving as president of courts-martial and boards of various kinds, such as supervising the buying of cavalry horses.

Libbie Custer, or the general's "little turtle dove", must have been watching for his return, since she met us at the door. She hugged her husband, and also gave Ludlow an affectionate hug, then looked at me just as the general had.

"General Terry's ward," Custer said, "and Spike's right-hand man."

Libbie was Army-wise enough to read the significance of that "General Terry's ward" comment. She gave me a smile that would have baked cookies, and took my hand. "We'll put you up, here, with us. You can share Tom's room." She might have added: "If you don't mind a few rattlesnakes in cages around the place." Tom was at least as eccentric as his older brother. I couldn't imagine in those days how anyone as gentle and refined by nature as Libbie Custer managed to put up with the Custer boys. Now I can, but only after a long life of learning about people. Beneath that sugar-coated exterior was a spirit wilder and tougher than any of them. I wasn't so young a boy that I didn't fall immediately in love with her, and it was to be a lifetime affair.

I've read just about everything that's been published about Custer and his coterie of associates, many who loved and admired him, and more who hated his guts. It's mostly speculation. None of the recent writers who have gained reputations as authorities on Custer and the Last Stand are equipped to understand doodly-squat about Custer. They blow a lot of smoke, anyhow. There is always a kernel of fact, but a lot of it misses the target by one hundred and eighty degrees.

What they all miss, even his contemporaries, except the select few who were welcome in the Custer inner circle, is that they were a hell of a lot of fun to be around.

Tom Custer, who had earned two Congressional Medals of Honor in the Civil War, was closest to Autie and a lieutenant in the 7th Cavalry, commanding a company. He showed up, coming off duty, just after I was escorted into the Custers' quarters.

Libbie introduced us, not forgetting to mention me being General Terry's ward, as though that would cut any ice with Tom. After I got to know Tom Custer, I'd bet that he'd as soon have thrown General Terry into the Missouri River as look at him.

He looked me over pretty close and said: "How old are you?"

I said: "Fifteen or so, I guess."

"What do you mean, you guess?"

"I'm an orphan and I can't remember."

I noticed a change come over Tom right away. Whatever you say about the Custers, they all had great big fat hearts ready to sympathize with anyone in a jam or having a hard time.

"Well," Tom said, "if you're fifteen, you're pretty good-sized for your age. But too young for me to talk you into jinin' the cavalry, I guess."

Libbie interrupted us, saying: "I hope you won't mind us bunking Mister Ballard in your room."

I loved that, mister, and she knew I would.

Tom grinned. "Do you snore pretty loud, kid?"

I didn't know if he was serious or not, and said: "I don't know."

He laughed. "Well, I snore. And I'll tell you if you do first thing in the morning. C'mon upstairs and I'll show you our digs."

Libbie said: "I'll have someone set up a cot."

Before we could get upstairs, there was a hell of a commotion in the front room and very shortly a black cat shot by us and headed up the stairs, closely followed by two greyhounds.

I heard Libbie yell: "Autie, someone let your hounds in! Get them out of here! They just chased Stonewall upstairs!"

The general headed upstairs, saying: "C'mon, Tom, and help me round them up."

Everyone had cats in those days to keep down the mouse and rat population. Stonewall, named for Stonewall Jackson, was a first-rate mouser. We found him in Tom's room on top of the chiffonier, looking very owlish. I wondered how often that happened and figured it probably happened about once a week, at least. I tried to reach up and scratch Stonewall's chin. He took a bat at me and hissed. He wasn't ready to be babied yet after having his dignity threatened.

I had a comfortable feeling that I was going to like it around there. I might not have if Tom had had his box of rattlesnakes on the dresser, which I learned he sometimes did. They had mysteriously disappeared. Libbie was the prime suspect. But I discovered all that later.

Tom flopped out on his bed and stretched. "You got a suitcase or such?" he asked.

"Got a duffel bag."

"Let's go find it, and then I'll get you a horse you can ride. I don't reckon you brought one out from Saint Paul." He was being funny, but I didn't know it.

Army officers owned their own string of horses. Tom had several. We went down to the stables and picked out one for me.

"I reckon you can ride," he said matter-of-factly.

"I don't fall off, if that's what you mean."

"I got just the horse for you, then," he said. "We'll saddle him up and you can try him out."

Tom told the stable sergeant: "Bring out Buns."

The stable sergeant led out the horse Tom indicated and saddled him up in the pen behind the stable. It wasn't hard to tell why they called him Buns. He had an outsize set of rear quarters. He was big all around—about sixteen hands—and sturdy, an ideal cavalry horse.

"Get on, kid," Tom said. "You'll like a McClellan saddle if you've never used one."

The fact of the matter was I'd never ridden much before I went out on a survey to the Canadian border with Captain Ludlow. I was far from a horseman, but I was strong and quick, and it was a good thing. I'd no sooner settled in the saddle and didn't even have my foot in the right stirrup when Buns and I headed skyward. I grabbed the saddle front and back and hung on and gripped like hell with my legs. I thought my teeth were going to come loose when I hit the ground on the first jump; I was lucky I didn't bite my tongue. It seemed like a half hour that I fought to stay on through one jump after another, till finally I felt the damned horse tiring out. Finally he stopped bucking and decided to run. I never had got hold of the reins and was lucky they weren't the split kind like cowboys use. These had been on and off Buns' neck while he bucked, but they had whipped back on when he finished his last buck. I finally was able to grab them and tried to pull him in. A lot of good that did. He headed for the fence and took it in one jump, me hanging onto the saddle for dear life. I was still in it when he headed for the high ground at a flat-out run. He must have made five miles before I could circle him back. By then I felt like I'd been dragged through a knothole. My legs felt like rubber, but I was determined to stay on if it killed me.

By the time I got him turned around, I noticed a rider coming after me at a high lope. It was Tom Custer. He pulled up alongside when at last I got Buns down to a walk. Tom didn't say a word for quite a while. Finally he said: "Funny, that old horse never did that before. Or did you decide to take him out for a little run?"

I'd been around long enough to say: "I'll just bet he never did that before."

Tom kept a straight face. "No, sir," he said. "That's the horse I keep for ladies from the East."

I told myself—*Sure it is.*—but was content to let it go at that.

The stable sergeant was waiting when we got back, sitting on the fence, smoking a stubby pipe that cavalrymen called a "dinky dudeen". He got down and took my horse by the bridle while I got off. I didn't know enough about tack yet to know they'd left the curb strap off the bridle and, besides, the bit was only a split snaffle. It left me about as much chance of pulling in Buns as I had of flying. A number of other troopers were around as well, pretending to be grooming horses, but watching us. I'm sure they were in on the "sell".

Tom said: "The kid is quite a rider."

The stable sergeant looked me over carefully, his face expressionless, but I'd bet he and Tom did this to every greenhorn that showed up. He said: "So I noticed."

"Tell the kid," Tom said to the sergeant, "that this horse has never done that before. He doesn't seem to believe me."

The old soldier grinned. "Then he probably wouldn't believe me, either, Lieutenant."

In other words, he didn't exactly say yes and he didn't exactly say no.

41

I judge this wasn't the first indoctrination of that kind, since the general met us on the porch when Tom brought me back, looking me over for signs of dusty or ripped clothes and a strawberry or two on my face.

"Where have you two been? Libbie is about to have supper set on."

Tom said: "I picked out a horse the kid can ride."

The general had a gleam in his eye when he asked me: "Does the horse suit you? Tom doesn't know a thing about horses. I told him to give you Buns since he's a ladies' horse."

I managed to say: "Buns is a little hard to get started, but I'll make out. Maybe I can get me a pair of spurs."

"I'll lend you a pair of mine," Tom said.

Then they both laughed like hell. This was an old gag with them, and I'd passed the test better than anyone they'd ever run across. Most didn't get beyond picking themselves out of the horse turds in the corral. Right there I got to be a bragging point for the Custers. I heard them telling a lot of people about me. I figured: *Now, if I can just manage to kill an Indian chief or a grizzly bear, bare-handed, I'll probably get to be a member of the family.*

Dinner at the Custers' was quite an affair. They had a black lady cooking for them, and the general's orderly, Burkman, acted as butler, more or less, and helped her serve. What a butler. He was born in Pennsylvania's Appalachian district, the cradle of feuding Southern mountain stock. He loved both the general and Libbie and was loyal as that kind can be. Libbie called him Old Nutriment behind his back, since he managed to chuck grub away at an alarming rate whenever he got the chance. I judge not many leftovers were ever heated over with Burkman on duty.

Chapter Five

The next morning I was congratulating myself on having fit in pretty well and having passed the necessary initiation tests, when someone grabbed me from behind as I headed over toward the stables. The next thing I knew I was on the ground, flat on my back, and Tom Custer was straddling me, pulling my ears, and mussing my hair.

He said: "You gotta learn to be quick and wary out here. Suppose I'd been a Sioux?" He got off me and gave me a hand up.

A great notion grabbed me. I'd learned to be a rough-and-tumble fighter in the gutter in St. Paul. Tom wasn't all that much bigger than me and he wasn't expecting me to put up a fight, so I tripped him, pounced on his back, and ground his face in the dirt good, then jumped up and ran.

The general had come out after us, took in the whole affair, and then laughed like hell. Tom took out after me, but I could also run like a deer, and he didn't even get close. That must have graveled him since the Custer boys all thought they could run some. Finally he gave it up, and I figured it was safe to come back.

"C'mere, Ballard," the general motioned to me.

I came over. He looked me up and down. I wondered if I was in for it for assaulting an Army officer. Finally the general said: "You're going to fit in here like a glove, kid. I aim to keep you alive till you're old enough to join the cavalry. Tom,

43

here, is getting along and not able to take care of himself, I notice, and I might give you his company if I can get you a commission. Or maybe I'll just assign you to him as a sort of keeper, to help him hobble around and keep him out of trouble."

Tom Custer said—"In a pig's eye."—but he laughed and clapped me on the back. "You're OK, Tom," he said to me. "You even got a good, respectable name."

"But we'll have to call him Tom-Two from now on," the general added, "so we don't get you two mixed up."

Later, Captain Ludlow, who had seen the last part of the affair, told me: "You just made two of the best friends anybody could ever have. They'll look out for you."

How true that was he could hardly know. Autie looked out for me until his last five minutes, but that's getting ahead of my story.

Before we left on our expedition, I learned something else that I needed to know. I wasn't exactly eavesdropping, but I'd just come downstairs and was about to go into the parlor when I saw Libbie and the general already there, and hesitated. They obviously hadn't heard me. Libbie was at the window with the curtain pulled aside slightly and she was saying: "There goes that crude oaf."

"Who?" he asked, coming over.

"Captain Benteen, who else?"

They both looked out and watched. I could just see around the two at the window and I judged they were referring to an officer just passing, leading a company of cavalry.

She said: "Why don't you have Phil send him to Fort Mojave, or somewhere? He'd do it if you asked."

I didn't yet know who the Phil she had referred to was, but learned it was General Phil Sheridan. He'd have done anything either of those two asked, if it was within reason and didn't get out to the public. Fort Mojave was within reason. It was an Army joke. If someone screwed up, the saying was: "Send him to Fort Yuma, and, if he screws up there, then there's always Mojave as a last resort." It was the garden spot of the Army posts, far up the Colorado River in the middle of nowhere.

Custer shook his head. "I can't spare Benteen. He's a fighter."

"Someday you'll regret it," she responded.

That's as much interference as I ever heard her offer in military affairs, but there was a note in her voice that scared me, like she was telling the future. She hated Benteen and would later have reason to hate him with a passion, and detest even his memory long after he was gone, until the day she died. I can't say that I blame her. I observed in time that being a fighter was Benteen's only redeeming trait. The day would come when—I'm certain as night follows day—he tried to have me put out of the way for knowing too much.

I have a full set of photographs taken of this expedition to the Black Hills, having managed to get my hands on them since I got to know the photographer we took along. His name was Illingworth and he worked in St. Paul, on and off, for years after the Indian wars were over. That was when I headquartered there as a construction engineer for the Great Northern. My having the pictures is sort of funny since Spike Ludlow didn't do nearly so well along that line with Illingworth. Ludlow finally sued him for the Army to get the six sets of pictures he had contracted to make. But Ludlow didn't get them, as I recall, unless he bought those made into postcards. Illingworth sold selected pictures to the public for years. Ludlow was probably happy to hear that Illingworth blew his own brains out years later.

Why am I telling you this? I don't know. I guess, as the saying goes: "With this sort of information and two bits you can get a cup of coffee almost anywhere."

On the other hand, you can never tell what's important to history. And I'm not about to leave out background that might be necessary to get at what frontier editors would have called "the true inwardness" of the situation that led to Custer's Last Stand.

The few publicly known incidents that stand out in my memory of the Black Hills expedition aren't the usual ones you read about. Nonetheless, I think they're the most interesting part of the affair, or, at least, the most pertinent. They have to do with the individuals I met and what I learned from them, or about them. The really interesting things I learned, of course, are not public knowledge.

The best secret I discovered was that there was a large land scheme afoot, not over town sites as was so often the case in the West, but a grab for what are today whole states. The players weren't small-time schemers, either. At the top of the list was a well-known American named Ulysses S. Grant who had a job coveted by most politicians. He was President of the U.S. and a Republican. He'd come out of the Civil War hailed as the savior of the Union with an unblemished record. This didn't last long after he got in over his head in politics. Others were major politicians of the time who were Grant's cronies, in most cases.

Inside the Army, and having a part in the scheme, were Grant's most trusted subordinates during the war: General William Sherman, a notorious Indian hater among other things, who saw the best resolution of the "Indian problem" as killing them all; General Phil Sheridan, famous for his remark that "the only good Indian is a dead one"; and Generals Crook and Terry, who were Sheridan's subordinates as department commanders whose commands bordered on the land being sought which was then known as The Great Sioux Reservation. Regardless of their personal feelings, the latter two wanted to wear a second star again as they had during the war. Their three superiors were the keys to that.

The destination of the 1874 "exploratory" expedition under Custer was the Black Hills, reputed to be the Sacred of Sacreds of Sioux lands, called by them *Paha Sapa*. Custer was merely at the end of the land-grabbing chain and had little to say about the matter. He followed orders. My observations indicate that his sympathies were with the Indians. That was the case with many Army officers who had had direct dealings with them. Of course, Custer also wanted to wear stars again, but I think if he had had to leave the frontier to wear them and take a department back East, he'd have thought a long while before accepting.

My first inkling of all this was the remark that Custer had made to Ludlow about the long-range objective, which was to establish Army forts in the Sioux Territory "to protect them". Oddly enough that had been the stated mission of the Army in the 1830s when the Eastern Indians were all forcibly moved West onto lands they were to hold "as long as the grass grows and the rivers run". At that time the land onto which they were moved was termed the Great American Desert, deemed useless for agriculture and not apt to attract whites. That dream lasted until 1854, when Kansas and Nebraska became territories and were opened to legal settlement. Illegal settlement had been going on for a number of years, ever since a few hardy souls learned that the Great American Desert was actually an agricultural paradise in parts of it now known as the wheat belt. The passage of the Homestead Act during the Civil War, which offered almost free land to the host of footloose veterans who flooded West after the war, doomed the Indians' lands and the Indians as well. It was only a matter of time. I came on the scene to witness the last act and the final descent of the curtain on that stupendous drama.

I have to conclude it was a splendid experience, but only since I can look back on it, which is to say I survived. The only part I'd just as soon have passed up was getting run over by General Terry's team in the first place, but, as you know, if that hadn't happened, I wouldn't have had a ticket to a live historical performance.

Two characters whose names seldom get top billing in the land grab are Clement Lounsberry and Nate Knappen. They were nominally newspapermen, but the former was a lot more than that, and the latter, little older than I was, had to have been one of the most fascinating and mysterious frontier characters that I met. And I met him before we left Fort Lincoln, while I was riding Buns around, taking in the spectacle of a major Army expedition getting organized to depart on a campaign.

By this time Buns was a little more manageable, mainly since I'd found out about the curb strap affair. In addition I had got hold of a reasonably severe spade bit from the stable sergeant. (As it happened, it was the bit that Tom Custer *always* used on Buns. Are you surprised? I wasn't after I'd been clued in. "Clued" is one of the really great expressions I learned from my World War II G.I. buddies. It says a lot.) Anyhow, Buns only tried to pitch me off once a day—every morning—and we were becoming fast friends—he being quite a bit faster than me, come to think of it.

Buns had a lot of curiosity about things, just like a nosy person. I finally acquired him, and I'll tell you how later. He got me out of the mess at the Little Big Horn, and I didn't get back to St. Paul for quite a while after the fight.

I first met Nate Knappen when Buns got a nosy fit and told me he wanted to go look over a bunch of men gathered at their breakfast fire. He had a habit of coming up to a group and obviously asking: "What are you fellows doing, if you don't mind my butting in?" I owned Buns for years, till the day he died, and anytime I was working on something outside where he could join me, he'd tiptoe up and look over my shoulder to see what I was doing, such as pounding a nail or something. And he invariably asked: "What are *we* doing?" He was a great one with the editorial *we*.

That morning the little bunch of men around the fire looked me over as though I was interrupting a confidential confab, and I probably was. Nate Knappen sized me up briefly, then looked over Buns a little longer than he had me, noting his good points and commenting: "That's a fine horse."

In those days everyone noticed horses. Even a Western village schoolmarm could identify every horse in a community at a half mile, so I wasn't surprised at his interest in my horse. It was a horse era.

"Belongs to General Custer's brother Tom," I said.

"I know," Nate said, which emphasized my point about people knowing horses by sight in those days.

"You a friend of Tom Custer?"

"I guess."

He grinned, getting interested. "What do you mean, you guess?"

"Well, I just met him a couple of days ago, but I guess he's a good enough friend by now to lend me a horse."

By then the others were taking notice, sensing that Knappen was fishing for information, like all newsmen did, though I didn't yet know he was a newsman.

Knappen said: "Tom lends that horse to a lot of people." He laughed out loud. "You must be quite a rider."

I wasn't one to brag, but thought I'd better say something since he was trying to be friendly. "I'm getting a lot better since Tom loaned me Buns."

Knappen laughed again. "Old Buns has dumped just about everybody that ever visited the Custers. They sort of use him for entertainment, you might say."

It was my turn to laugh. "I entertained the hell out of 'em, if that's the case, but the son-of-a-bitch didn't dump me. I was too quick for him."

By then the whole group, four of them besides Knappen, were interested in me and Buns. I can see how Knappen got to be a first-rate newsman even though he wasn't yet twenty. He knew how to draw a person out.

I've got an old news clipping that explains what he was doing in the Black Hills. It's sort of frayed and yellow, but I can still read it. In pencil, I wrote in the margin that it's from the June 24th, 1874 Bismarck *Tribune*, and the article says: **N.H. Knappen lays his scalp on the altar of the *Tribune* and goes with Custer to the Black Hills as our special reporter.**

That was no joke about his scalp. In those days the town of Bismarck had only been carved out of Sioux country for a couple of years, since the Northern Pacific reached the Missouri River. That naturally resulted in a town sprouting, as towns always did along railroad lines, especially where the lines crossed a river. Undoubtedly the article was written by the *Tribune*'s owner and editor, Clement Lounsberry, who knew the Sioux weren't too happy about the assumption that it was no longer their country.

"Light, and have some coffee," Knappen invited. "If you ain't et, pitch in with us. I'll git you a plate."

How typically Western that was. He'd never seen me before but was willing to whack up their grub with me. Of course, we can't forget he was a newsman on a "fishing" expedition, but almost anyone else would have done the same in those days. How I miss that old-time hospitality. You'll hunt a long time to find much of it around Los Angeles today, or in any other city, I suspect.

I tied Buns to the wheel of their wagon, and joined them. I'd eaten an hour or so before with the Custers, but, when I was young, I had an appetite like a bear just out of hibernation. Buns immediately set about untying himself so he could take a little run, but I'd already learned his tricks and had a snap fastener on the end of a leather hitching strap. The cavalry usually kept both a halter and bridle on their horses—a good idea that I adopted all my life, when I still had to depend on horses to get around. Buns didn't look too happy until I fed him half a pancake.

Knappen introduced me to his group. They included Ross and McKay, the two practical miners who were going with Custer. The other two were Charlie Reynolds, a guide, and George Bird Grinnell, who later became famous as an Indian authority. He was a professor from Yale, but he wasn't dressed like one. I'd have taken him for a teamster. We shook hands all around. Charlie Reynolds, known as Lonesome Charlie, got to be famous in his own way by getting killed with Custer at the Little Big Horn. He was Custer's favorite scout, along with a Ree Indian named Bloody Knife, who was killed not far from Lonesome Charlie the same day. I was rubbing elbows with some star-crossed people from the Custer saga, but had no idea of it at the time.

I was getting used to being accepted as a man by men. It was a time and place that took you for what you could do, and

51

I was engaged in a man's business. That bunch figured anyone Tom Custer loaned a horse to, especially *that* horse, must be OK. And in a country where that "laying your scalp on the altar" business was no joke, kids got to be *men* pretty quick. There were cases where kids, say a six- or eight-year-old boy, or even a girl, had killed Indians when they attacked a ranch or settlement. People teethed on guns because they knew that your gun was what kept you and those around you alive. Women were grounded in that as well. A good wife, at the very least, knew how to load the extra musket for you, and had the guts to shoot a redskin if he busted into your cabin. But it wasn't like the movies where an apple-cheeked heroine minces around wide-eyed, with her fist balled up over her open mouth, ignoring the gun lying on the ground right in front of her that the hero and the villain are fighting to get hold of, while peeing down her leg every time they wrestle up to the edge of the inevitable cliff. You've all seen it over and over, I guess, straight from the pen of some Bronx screenwriter.

Anyhow, back to that morning in 1874. We finished eating and were sitting around, smoking and drinking coffee, when Knappen asked me if I fished. I did. Always loved to, having been around the Mississippi where fishing got us the only thing that street kids had to eat sometimes, and we did it even in winter when we fished through the ice. "Sure do," I told him.

He said: "If old Tom Custer and his big brother can spare you, I'll take you fishing for some of the best sport you've ever had."

"I don't exactly work for the Custers," I said. "In fact, I work for Captain Ludlow, but we aren't doing much right now. I don't reckon anyone will miss me."

That's how I ended up on a fishing expedition I expected

would be up the Missouri a ways above the fort. It was fairly safe out there by then, but I noticed that Knappen had a Henry Rifle in his saddle boot and a .45 Colt strapped around him. I had just got my own rifle—an Army Springfield—and had a pocketful of shells. The 7th Cavalry had been issued new carbines before leaving on campaign, and I bought one of the old ones for $2 from the quartermaster. I was riding a McClellan saddle and had the Springfield hung on the saddle ring.

It turned out that I wasn't being taken on the kind of fishing expedition I expected, but that suited me OK, too. In those days I was up for almost anything. That's how I learned a lot I'd have been as well off not knowing, then or ever. It was the clue to what the whole expedition was about and probably what got Knappen killed for knowing too much, a couple of years later. I knew as much as he did, but no one was wise to me. Nonetheless, I was in a ticklish spot for years on account of that morning.

When we were out of hearing of anyone, Knappen asked: "How'd you like to earn a little extra money on this expedition?"

It didn't take me long to bite on that. "How?"

"Just keeping your ears open. I've got a little fund from my newspaper to pay for information."

I thought that over. "As long as I'm not telling tales on my friends, it sounds OK to me."

"Nothing like that. Just big news about events."

"Such as what?" I couldn't think of a thing along that line that I might run across.

"You might learn a lot being around Custer. He likes to make it into the newspapers. All officers do. It's how they get promoted in the long run."

I thought that over. "Like I said, as long as it isn't carrying tales." I thought of what I'd heard between Custer and Libbie about Benteen.

"Naw. The kind of news about what big men may have said to Custer. No one will know where we got it. We always say 'a source close to', or something like that."

We were riding toward the river while we talked. He led the way to the ferry.

"We goin' fishin' on the other side?" I asked.

"You might say that." He laughed. "I want you to meet my boss, Mister Lounsberry. He's over in Bismarck. He'll OK putting you on the payroll. He heard you're close to General Terry, too."

"Where did he hear that?" I blurted, surprised.

"Hell, in a place like Fort Lincoln everyone knows every-thing about everybody sooner or later. Usually sooner."

Lounsberry had been a newspaper editor in St. Paul, and knew General Terry pretty well. But Terry would be careful around a newsman, making sure he learned only what he wanted him to. I suppose that's where I was to come in. But it was really accidental in the first place. Knappen had no idea I'd wander up to his camp, but he was quick on the uptake and saw my potential right away. He knew his boss would buy in. On the other hand, if I hadn't stumbled into him, he may have looked me up—probably would have.

We stepped aside for an Army officer coming out of the newspaper office, accompanied by a sergeant. I noticed that the officer gave me a good looking over, but I just figured he might know who I was and naturally wonder what I was doing there. I recalled Knappen's remark about everyone at the fort knowing everyone's business "usually sooner". I hadn't got a good look at Benteen when the Custers were watching him out their front window, or I'd have known who the officer was.

After those two brushed by, Knappen led the way inside. The Bismarck *Trib*'s office was nothing to brag about, filling all of a board shack about twenty feet square. It was crowded with a couple of desks, the press, and composing table, and even a cot in the corner, with a chamber pot under it. And let's not forget the indispensable spittoons.

Knappen interrupted the man at one of the desks with: "Clem, I brung us a treasure, I reckon."

I figured from that "Clem" that the man had to be Lounsberry and was a little surprised that a kid not much older than I was felt free to call him that.

He looked me over with a pair of shrewd eyes, as though to say: "Well, treasures come in all sorts of packages. We'll see."

Knappen introduced us.

Lounsberry cut out a lot of conversational underbrush in a few words by saying: "When you get back with General Terry, tell him hello for me."

If Knappen hadn't prepared me for that remark with his clue about everyone learning who you were pretty quick, I'd have ended up with my mouth open. "I'll do that," was all I said.

"He and I are great friends," Lounsberry said, leading me to wonder how that had happened since he sure didn't look like the sort that the Terrys associated with by choice. I learned later that even General Terry's kind played to newsmen, and the reason was that, when it came to getting that first or second star, good publicity impressed the President who made nominations to Congress.

"I remember when the general's buggy ran over you," Lounsberry said. "We put a little item in the paper. You fell into a shithouse and came out smelling like a rose. You'll go a long ways with Terry's help if you don't make any mistakes."

I nodded, wondering what kind of mistakes he meant. I'd

already skipped school, but didn't have the mother wit or nerve to ask him what kind of mistakes. Pity. Innocently telling the truth at the wrong time, on the assumption that a pious man like Terry would appreciate it, was a mistake I least considered.

Knappen said: "I told Tom we'd pay him a little if he came up with information."

"Good." Lounsberry looked at me. "I guess that's OK with you?"

"I told Nate it was OK as long as I wasn't squealing on someone or giving away secrets on my friends."

"Hell, no! Nothing like that!"

In fact, that was exactly what he'd have liked best, not necessarily to put in the paper, but to *leave out* as a favor to someone, so he could hold it over their head. I may have suspected that, but can't recall. I do recall that I was too young and dumb to ask about the salary scale, but then I couldn't think of anything I'd ever have to sell to them in the first place. Little did I know.

After a few more polite words, Lounsberry ignored me. He reached into a desk drawer and drew out a wrapped package and handed it to Knappen, saying: "Here's a little early Christmas present . . . a couple of extra boxes of Forty-Five shells. You might need them."

After we were back across the Missouri, riding toward the fort, Knappen said: "I probably shouldn't tell you what's really in that package, but it's too rare to keep. Promise you won't tell a soul?"

"I learned not to be lippy long ago," I said.

He was right. He *shouldn't* have told me, and it was rare. Smart as he was, his mouth probably got him killed young. God knows to whom else he told his "rare" secret.

He laughed boisterously. "Get this! We aim to publish the

56

news that there's gold in the grassroots out where we're going."

"Suppose there isn't?" I asked.

"There has to be. We aim to see that Bismarck is the biggest jumping-off spot to the new Eldorado."

"So?"

"So, if there isn't gold in the grassroots, I've got a package full of it to plant there."

I knew it wasn't honest, but, when you've been down and out and close to starving, honest doesn't mean all that much to you. Especially if your ox doesn't get gored in some scam. Actually I thought it was pretty funny.

"Remember," he said, "you promised not to tell."

"I won't forget."

I never have told up till now when it won't hurt a soul. I even found out whose idea it was at the very top, but I think I'll just take that one to the grave with me. That might hurt a soul.

Chapter Six

Custer's 1874 campaign to the Black Hills was my introduction to the Wild West, a place I learned to love. It was a young man's country. I wouldn't want to go back and live my adventures there over, unless I could be young again. I don't even want to take one last look at the country I pioneered in. It's full of people. Civilized. Thinking of those long gone days and the big, silent, virgin land only reminds me how tragic it is to grow old. I could afford to take a final look without stepping outside a limousine, but . . . no thanks. Doing it that way would be a lot easier, but not as much fun as when Buns was my limousine.

While Custer's expedition was getting together, I used to ride up on the hills beyond the fort where I could see wagons every direction I looked. Long parks of them. And troop tents pitched in orderly rows. Herds of mules, horses, and the cattle we were going to take along to butcher *en route* were also spread around on the prairie and close herded to see that the Indians didn't run them off.

A picture is undoubtedly worth a thousand words, but no picture could bring out the main dimension. Noise. The braying of mules and bellowing of cattle. Horses added their whinnies, day and night, and I assumed they had something on their minds to say, but could never be sure what it was except for Buns when he rumbled deep in his throat when I was feeding him, suggesting I hurry up about it.

Horses have buddies they yell to when they get separated.

A horse is a creature of habit and wants its friends around. They are herd critters and require at least one other horse to be happy, and preferably more, since a social group is their secondary resort for defense, rating right after running. When they see or even smell preying wild animals in the vicinity, they want to run off and, if they can't, take position back to back. Three or four or more will form a circle facing outward, to fight off an attack with teeth and striking forefeet.

The troopers were also social beasts for the most part. Loners like Paddy O'Toole were unusual, and like him were persons with above average self-sufficiency. Charlie Reynolds was one of those, and earned the name Lonesome Charlie as a result, not that he resented company if it wanted to join him, but I never saw him join others without being encouraged. The morning I met him with Knappen's group, he was probably in on the gold scheme. In any case, he was with the main participants, and he was the rider that carried the news out when gold was actually discovered.

Few on the frontier would have seen anything wrong with carrying such news, whether there was gold or not. They'd have laughed if the truth got out, though the Eastern newspapers opposed to the Grant Administration would have peed down their legs, as usual. The West loved jokes, the bigger the better, and seldom gave a damn who was hurt, or how many. The idea in this case was to get the damned Indians to hell out of the Black Hills, since, gold or not, the country was a paradise for raising livestock and good for farming along the streams or almost anywhere in wet years.

The feature of the landscape around the fort that lent charm to the whole gathering together of the Army expedition was the backdrop of the wide, looping Missouri River, which just at that time was running high due to snow melt in the mountains far upstream. It was the best season for freight to be carried up the river by steamboats, since a proper depth in the channel minimized the ever-present danger of grounding on sandbars. A good part of the supplies needed for that expedition came upriver by boats. The steamers were the familiar type that is associated in most minds only with the Mississippi—broad in the beam, shallow draft, and pushed by a stern wheel. They were slow but provided cheap transportation so that they competed with railroads for many years after the tracks had come West. Their fuel came cheap, being wood cut from the riverbanks, which gave rise to a trade for woodcutters along the river's banks, for years, as long as the steamer trade lasted.

I rejoined Captain Ludlow's crew as we started west. Paddy O'Toole was glad to see me, I could tell, though he tried not to show it. For the rest, it's hard to say if they had missed me or not. I remember them all, kept in touch with most of them until they died.

Paddy said: "I hear you've bin hobnobbin' with the mighty. You don't look any the worse for it."

He was grinning widely, and I didn't see much to say about it, so just grinned back. Finally I thought of something at least half bright to say, which was: "You ain't jealous, are you? I hobnob with the mighty back in Saint Paul, too."

"Different kind of mighty. This kind doesn't put on the dog . . . and they fight."

He knew I didn't mind him reflecting on the Terrys. I had grumbled about them to him often enough. When I told him about cotillion and my Little Lord Fauntleroy britches, I thought he'd wronged his drawers he laughed so hard.

"You goin' back to Saint Paul when we get back?" he asked.

"I reckon the general wants me to."

"How about you? What do you want to do? You're your own man now."

"I don't know for sure. I kinda think I'd like to study to be an engineer like Ludlow."

"And be an engineer in the Army?"

"I don't know for sure. It looks to me like Army officers do pretty well."

Paddy said: "The Army's a good place to be for a few years." I suspected that he meant if you were hiding out until the heat died down somewhere. Then he added: "But there's more money being a big bug in private life."

That may have been where the idea first popped into my mind that I could make my fortune as an engineer somewhere.

"Anyhow," he said, concluding what was a long speech for him, "schoolin' never hurt anyone. I'd have got more myself, but Pa was always beatin' up Ma, so I killed him and had to run away."

He said it so matter-of-factly that I thought he must be kidding, but I looked him over and concluded that maybe he wasn't. I thought I'd let that one slide in any case and never pressed him about it. He was sure capable of killing. In those days it's doubtful they'd have sent him to jail if he had killed a drunken wife-beater, especially when it was his own ma that got beat, and most of the beating kind were drunks.

The main point of my telling you about this 1874 picnic to the Black Hills is to tell you about a few other people, like Paddy, who were involved at last in Custer's death. One of them, in my view, contributed to the unnecessary slaughter of a great part of the 7th Cavalry at the Little Big Horn a couple of years later. This chief villain in the piece is Captain Frederick W. Benteen, who hated Custer from their first meeting in 1867, and grew to dislike him more and more with the passage of their almost ten years together.

We were out as far as the Cannonball River when I got my first taste of Benteen's style. I told you I'd seen him leaving the newspaper office in Bismarck and got a "look" from him then. I still wonder what he was doing there. Was he in on the scheme to plant gold if need be? In any case, I am certain he tried to have me killed a few years later to preserve his reputation, because he suspected I knew more than would be good for it, but that wasn't about gold.

At the Cannonball River camp, the men were swimming in the river, both officers and enlisted men. A funny affair happened there that I've never seen in anybody's memoirs. All of the Custers were in the river taking a bath, and I was with them, since I was off duty and spent a lot of time with them when I could. By this time the youngest brother, Boston, had joined the expedition. I liked him as much as I did Tom. He was up for anything. It ran in the family blood, and included their old father as I learned later. They used to tease him unmercifully and play jokes on him, and, I have no doubt, if he'd been along, he'd have been with us, bare-assed, involved in the fun.

Anyhow, someone got the idea that we ought to run a race in the buff. In view of the ever-present cactus, boots were the only permissible attire. So we lined up and set off cross-country. The general wasn't one to be left behind in anything and was ahead of his brothers, but I outran them all. When we finally settled down, puffing, he had a fiery look in his eye that suggested he didn't care to get bested by anyone, even in a foot race. But he managed to laugh, saying: "You remind me of a story Lincoln told me about the battle of Bull Run. There was a lot of 'Run' there as I well know, since I was there. Anyhow a bunch of spectators had come out from Washington to see us whip the Rebels, but it didn't come out that way. One of the Congressmen, who'd come out with a buggy, a picnic lunch, and some ladies, got separated from his transportation and was running full tilt when a rabbit got in his way. Lincoln couldn't help but laugh at most of his own jokes, and he was laughing when he told me . . . 'So the Congressman kicked the rabbit out of his way and said . . . ' "Git outta the way and let someone run that knows how." ' I guess you'd have suited Lincoln pretty well along those lines, kid."

About then Benteen came by with a fishing pole, and Tom Custer said: "Colonel Benteen"—he'd have said Fred, if he liked him—"why don't you set down your pole and come in and cool off."

Benteen eyed the whole group of us with a frosty look so much as to say it was what he expected from a bunch of un-soldierly bums who had never grown up. "I'd rather do a little pan fishing," he said, probably thinking that he ought to say something.

Tom Custer said: "Are you trying to hide something?" He wiggled his hips and his tool swung around, and it wasn't anything to be ashamed of. All the Custers were pretty well fixed in that department.

Benteen's face reddened, but he didn't say anything and went on his way.

"I'll bet he's got one of those short Rebel cocks," Tom said, loud enough for Benteen to hear him. "He's from Virginia."

That was too much for Benteen. He spun around, not giving a damn whether Tom was the commanding officer's brother or not, and that commander right there to boot. Besides, there was no rank off duty in such matters. He said: "Tom, how would you like to have me slap the shit out of you for having a big mouth?"

Tom grinned and asked: "With clothes on or this way?"

The general didn't say a word. We have to remember he had graduated a month late from West Point for practically refereeing a fist fight when he was on guard duty and bound by regulations to stop it. As a matter of fact, Captain Ludlow had been one of the fighters at that time, which made him and the general all the closer.

Benteen dropped his fishpole and said: "Any way you want it."

It was a situation that had gone so far that a fight couldn't be ducked. Everyone within hearing came closer, and the crowd attracted others.

Tom approached Benteen, fists up and ready, and danced around him. He wasn't about to get too close until he wore down the bigger man. Benteen must have outweighed him by at least forty pounds. He took a roundhouse swing at Tom, and naturally Tom wasn't there when it swished by, since he'd danced away.

Benteen was already breathing hard. He was pushing forty, drank too much, like a lot of officers did, and he looked like he hadn't missed many meals in a long while.

"Fight like a man," Benteen suggested.

"How is that?" Tom asked. "Let a big mule like you get in a lucky kick? No way."

While he was talking, he suddenly chopped at Benteen and landed a punch on the side of his head that staggered him. Tom was strong and quick. It rocked Benteen and stung him into charging, just as Tom expected it would, and that rush got the bigger man another chop alongside his head as he blundered past. He turned and glared, standing spread-legged. He was beginning to sense that he was going to get shellacked by a lot smaller man. His face was red as a tomato. "Goddamn you, you yellow little shit ass. If I could get my hands on you, I'd break every bone in your fuckin' Custer body."

At that Custer's face turned white. "This has gone about far enough," he snapped. "You're both under arrest. And, Tom, apologize to the Captain Benteen."

At first Tom looked at his brother as though he'd lost his mind, then he read the tone of voice and look in his eyes.

A lot has been written pro and con about Custer, but I've got to say that surely the acid test of command is to sound commanding while standing out on the prairie wearing nothing but a pair of cavalry boots. Autie passed muster with flying colors.

"Do as I say!" Custer ordered. "You started it and made some ungentlemanly remarks."

"So did he!" Tom protested.

"You asked for them."

Tom hung his head like a little boy caught in the cookie jar. "All right." He turned to Benteen and said: "Accept my humble apologies, Captain Benteen, on behalf of the fuckin' Custers."

At that everyone laughed, even Benteen.

"Forget it," he said.

He probably thought he was getting off easy, since he hadn't actually been whipped by a smaller man in front of the whole regiment.

What missed everyone was that Custer actually won that fight without even being in it. He'd maneuvered Benteen into the rôle of a beggar by giving him an out, and showed the Custers as gentlemen who were big enough to admit a mistake and apologize for a transgression. This was all the more so, since almost everyone knew that Benteen hated the Custers' guts and didn't really deserve an apology. It certainly didn't do anything to diminish Benteen's hatred for Autie, or for any of them.

I noticed that Custer didn't suggest that Tom shake hands with Benteen. Maybe he thought the bigger man would grab him and try to get even, which would force him to take a stronger official position. Custer's final words were: "All right, you two are no longer under arrest."

No one who knew all the parties and their feud thought that was the end of it.

The only part of the expedition that mattered to me, come to think of it, was the by-play of the actors such as that. I met a lot of the other officers of the 7th and those attached to it. The one I liked best was Captain Tom French who had come up from Fort Rice with Benteen as one of his company commanders. His first sergeant, Ryan, and I became good friends over the years, mostly by mail. Ryan hated Benteen's guts with good reason and, according to Ryan, so did Captain French. But the latter never showed it, except once.

French and Ryan were with Benteen a couple of years later when they rode up and found Custer's dead body. According to Ryan, Benteen said: "There the son-of-a-bitch lies. He's fought his last battle."

French blew up and said: "Fred, I ought to make you skin that back or blow your god-damn' head off! He deserves better than that and you know it!"

Benteen just looked at him, got red, then rode away.

"I wish he had blown his head off," Ryan said. "I know I'd have liked to. I think the bastard suspected that French would have got him if it came down to it, one on one. French was the closest thing to a gunfighter that we had in the Seventh."

Chapter Seven

Obviously my Terry connection was behind a kid like me being able to rub elbows with the mighty. It was naturally uncomfortable since I had no background to handle such an unexpected kick upstairs. But the reason I met the mightiest of them all, shortly after the foot race between me and the Custers, had no direct relation to Terry. It was because the mighty fellow had seen me run.

He didn't care who the hell I was, and, to him, General Terry was small potatoes. The reason he was interested in me was that he was a gambler. That's something that has never come out about him, though it should be obvious from his record. His old man was a hell of a gambler, too, which historians have seemed to deëmphasize, if they have the mother wit to dance around the subject at all.

Spike Ludlow got hold of me later the day I'd beat the Custer boys in the foot race and said: "Kid, the President's son wants to talk to you."

I must have looked as surprised as I was and sounded as ignorant as they come, when I asked: "President of what?"

"President of the United States!" he said, no doubt savoring my look of astonishment. My stomach grabbed me like it does when a cop puts a heavy hand on your shoulder.

"Am I in Dutch over something?" I asked. The first thought that always occurred to me in those days was that when someone important wanted to see me, it could only be because I'd done something wrong.

"Far from it. Come on over to his tent with me and find out for yourself."

Fred Grant looked a lot like his old man, and may have cultivated the similarity with the familiar clipped Grant beard. If you want to know what he looked like, a good likeness was made by Illingworth on that expedition. He's sitting at the front of a group of officers gathered around a banquet table laid out in the shade of a big tent, and the bottles on the table aren't full of cold water, either. He liked his nip, just like old U.S. did. Significantly Custer isn't in the picture. He was probably out hunting. Even Fred Grant might have hesitated to incur the Custer wrath by openly drinking and encouraging a group of Custer's officers to do it with him. On the other hand, he might have considered Custer small potatoes, too, just like Terry who was a mere brigadier general. Maybe not, since Custer still had a hell of a reputation then, even with Fred's old man, until he got on his blacklist a couple of years later. Few in the country didn't know who General Custer was, even though reduced to a mere lieutenant colonel in the postwar Army. Fred Grant was only twenty-four then, and not exactly cut in the pattern of Mars like his old man. Custer probably awed him.

Fred Grant and I looked each other over, he sitting in one of those folding canvas officer's chairs, me standing. He didn't invite me to sit down. Ludlow left after delivering me, maybe by prearrangement.

Grant said: "I saw you run. You're pretty fast."

I couldn't think of anything to say to that. It was true. If I'd ever thought about it, I'd have realized I'd never been beaten in a race with anyone in my class, or by some who were way out of it—including a few inspired matches against the St. Paul cops.

He continued to look me over, and I was getting uncomfortable and wishing I was somewhere else. Finally he said: "How would you like to make some money and have some fun at the same time?"

I've never had a thing against either money or fun.

"How?" I asked.

"Racing. Foot racing. Every company in the Army thinks it has someone that can run. They're always getting up races. The enlisted men can't afford horse racing, so they race each other. It's good for morale. They bet their heads off. They don't have a lot, but they bet everything they have."

I have no idea, even to this day, why he went to so much trouble to explain the situation. Maybe he thought I'd have some scruples against betting. As poor as I'd been for years, there were few things I had any scruples against, if I got some of the take.

"Would you mind if I set up some foot races with you against the company champs?" he asked.

"I'm game," I said, and regretted it pretty soon after thinking it over.

Just then fate sent Captain Benteen past Grant's tent.

"Hey, Fred!" Grant called to him.

Benteen came over and eyed me with a look that said: "What the hell is Grant doing with this mudsill?"

Grant indicated another chair, and Benteen sat down, straining its seams. Even then he was getting too heavy.

"I got a little proposition," Grant said. "You've got the regiment's champion baseball team and a few boys who think they can run." He let that hang in the air.

Benteen's face assumed a defensive wariness. He was jealous of the reputation of Company H's baseball team and had the mother wit to clue in to what Grant was driving at, with me standing there.

"There isn't a lot to occupy the men's minds on a campaign like this," Grant said. "I saw the kid here run and I'm backing him against the fastest man you can put up."

Benteen guffawed, then gave me a dirty look. "Hell, most of the team could trim him. The Custers can't run for sour owl shit! Beatin' them doesn't mean a thing."

Grant's face remained impassive. It sounded to me like maybe Benteen knew him pretty well to use that kind of language, but, on the other hand, I wondered if Grant didn't think Benteen was being insolent. True, he was only a few years out of West Point and, without family drag, would have been a junior second lieutenant. But he wasn't. He was a lieutenant colonel, on Sheridan's staff at that, and also sent along with Custer as an unofficial inspector general in all probability.

Grant said: "Well, Fred, that may be, so I'll make you a proposition. I'll put up ten bucks on the kid for every man you want to bring on to race against him."

There was no way in the world that Benteen could dodge such a proposition, especially after shooting his mouth off. He gave me another sour look, as though he was blaming me for the pickle he'd talked himself into. "You're on, Fred," he said. "When do you want this affair to come off?"

"Give it a couple of days for the word to circulate. There'll be a lot who'll want to bet on a race like that. I'll give half of what I make to the Regimental Morale Fund, and the kid gets the other half."

Benteen gave a genuine laugh for the first time. "What makes you so sure you'll make a dime?"

Grant grinned. "I'll make you a bet of a hundred bucks, right now, that the kid beats everyone you put up."

You can imagine how that made me feel. Suppose I lost? Benteen's mouth had got him into another pickle he couldn't very well eel out of.

"OK," he said, then added with bravado since he'd already put his foot in it: "Let's make it two hundred?"

You can believe that, by the next day, everyone on the expedition knew who I was. It was a situation naturally bound to get me into trouble. I can imagine how Benteen felt, since I was pretty queasy about the whole proposition myself. I was already thinking of stealing Buns and heading west, in case I lost.

It didn't help when Tom Custer came by and said: "Come on over to Autie's mess. We're going to feed you up good, so you'll have your strength for running. We're betting our whole taw on you. I even bet your horse against three hundred bucks from Benteen. Even bet my tobacco money and what I've been savin' for the collection plate the next time I go to church." He laughed like hell over that. Even today I'd bet that he hadn't been in a church for years, unless he went to squire some lady he had his hopes up about.

He may have been laughing, but you can bet I wasn't. I couldn't eat much of what Tom tried to stuff into me, and I couldn't sleep that night. It got worse during the couple of days before the match was set.

The horrible part of it was thinking that I might condemn my good old horse to having to suffer the likes of that "crude oaf" Benteen. I almost puked when I thought of it. I wondered how the hell Tom Custer could have put me in such a bind. If I lost, there was only one thing to do—steal Buns and cut for the mountains.

I was at the Custer supper table the night before the race was scheduled. We expected to reach the Grand River the next day and were planning on having the race the following morning. By then I was beginning to feel a little better. I'd actually been able to choke down some of the Custers' chuck, which must have given me some extra energy. I've got to say that even lieutenant colonels didn't do too badly for being waited on in the old Army. Charlie Reynolds and Bloody Knife kept the mess supplied with fresh meat, which consisted mostly of antelope, but along the rivers you could find elk, and even an occasional buffalo, although they ranged mostly west of the Little Missouri River. I had a pretty good appetite, since I'd been jogging alongside the column and, every once in a while, doing a hundred-yard sprint. They were going to have to bring on a real runner to beat me.

Fred Grant and Ludlow ate with General Custer, and the other members of our mess were Tom and Boston Custer, as well as some who came and went by invitation, such as Major Forsyth and Major Tilford, who commanded the two battalions or wings of the force, and the scientific people like Professors Marsh and Grinnell. They all treated me royally, and not like a kid except when the younger Custers wanted to rough-house with me.

My appetite, as I said, had picked up, and I was looking forward to supper until Grant asked me: "Have you ever run a mile?"

As it happened I had, but not as a regular thing. It wasn't my best distance. About two or three blocks with the cops behind me was my distance. I looked at him and asked: "Why? We ain't running over a couple of hundred yards are we?"

He said: "I'm afraid so. Maybe I got a little too generous, but Benteen said that, since his ball players are all short-distance runners who can put on a burst of speed with the best of them, he'd give us the advantage and make the course longer since only one of his men had to beat you to win the whole pot."

Custer broke in: "And you agreed to what?"

"A mile."

My stomach felt like it had a little turtle inside, swimming around.

It was on the tip of my tongue to blurt out—"What the hell did you do that for, you dumb son-of-a-bitch?"—but I knew that wouldn't have been the thing to say to the President's son, who was also a lieutenant colonel.

The look on Custer's face said it for me. And Tom, who would have spoken up to God, if he thought it was called for, said it out loud for all of us. "What the hell did you agree to that for?"

Grant sighed. "I know. I know. I shouldn't have. But it's done now. It's only money."

A voice inside me took over and blurted out: *Only money, my ass! It's Buns! My good old boy. I'll be goddamned if I lose him!* In my mind I was already headed for the Montana camps on a stolen horse. I'd thought of going even before I had a horse. Cotillion had helped, but I was also a poor boy who wanted to get rich.

Custer said: "Benteen is a fellow you can count on to play by the rules . . . as long as they're his rules. He's got a sergeant that can run like an Indian . . . uphill and down, all day." He looked at me and said: "It's up to you to put your heart into this."

As my World War II buddies would so aptly put it today: "No shit?"

That's how things stood when we reached the Grand and set up camp. Benteen and Grant laid out the racecourse. I couldn't eat a thing for supper and didn't sleep much that night. I felt like I was dreaming when we went out to the starting line. There were not only Benteen's contestants, but at least a man from every other company, and even a couple of teamsters had managed to be accepted to compete. One of them was a giant, at least six foot five tall, and built like a string bean. He looked like he could jump over sagebrush. Benteen tried to have him disqualified, but the impromptu race rules committee, which consisted of Majors Forsyth and Tilford, overruled him.

The course was marked with yellow streamers that were part of Ludlow's kit used for marking the location of surveying poles.

I lined up with the rest, feeling like an ant among elephants. The fellow next to me kept crowding over, pretending he didn't know I was there. Then they shot off the starting gun and I leaped away like a deer, almost. Someone held onto my shirttail. It was the fellow who had crowded me. He obviously wasn't there as a contestant, but to slow me down at the start. I wondered if anyone had seen the foul play. Almost the whole field was ahead of me. The whole thing was a blur in my mind as I determined to overtake and pass them all. I willed my legs to turn into pistons as on a locomotive and soon was passing runners all along the course. At about the halfway point, where Captain French was posted on a horse as the marker for the turning point, I had just about left the other runners behind me, except the lanky teamster and Benteen's Sergeant Salmon, which wasn't his real name, who was running like he didn't even know the ground was there.

By then my legs were getting tired, and the air trying to get into my lungs burned like fire. I thought—*I'm going to lose.*—and started planning what I'd steal to take along as rations when Buns and I cut out. But the inner voice butted in again, saying: *Just one damned minute. Don't forget asking God for a little help.* I started praying. That's when my second wind began to cut in, and my feet seemed to be flying like they weren't even attached to me.

I passed the teamster and heard him gasp out: "Go it, kid! It's up to you."

At least *he* wasn't a poor sport.

But when Sergeant Salmon heard my churning feet behind him, he put on an extra burst of speed.

I could see a bunch of people around the finish line, a hundred yards or so ahead, and thought: *God, if you love me, let me pour it on.* I pulled abreast of my opponent, then a little ahead, and I put my head down and charged, my knees almost hitting my chin. Just before the finish line I saw what looked like a spear flying at my legs from the right. I jumped whatever it was, tripped, and landed on my face just past the finish line, which was one of Ludlow's yellow ribbons stretched between stakes. I was barely conscious for a minute, trying to drag in enough breath to survive. Someone tried to pick me up, and I shook him off because I just wanted to lie there and rest, struggling to breathe.

Finally my surroundings settled down and swam into view. Paddy O'Toole picked me up and led me away, actually walking me down like a race horse to cool me off. I heard him say: "I knocked that son-of-a-bitch's teeth out."

It made no sense to me. I managed to say: "What?"

He said: "That asshole, Benteen, had one of his men at the finish line, and he tossed a long stick out of the brush to trip you. I come around behind him and knocked his teeth out. He's still over there in the brush, I imagine."

Then a press of bodies surrounded me, each one trying to congratulate me at the same time, and the foremost of them was Custer himself. He said: "You ran a helluva race, kid!" It was the only time, up till then, that I ever heard him come close to cussing. He was pounding me on the back, and then he even picked me up and swung me around. He was strong as a bull but didn't look it, being lean and slim.

Well, you may guess I was a hero to almost everyone on the expedition—except a few. It doesn't take a snake long to slither into the garden. Some troops thought they might not be able to outrun me, but that they could whip me with their fists, or wrestling. The day wasn't over when the first one of them tried me out. He caught me heading out into the brush to take a leak, just as we were pitching camp that night. He had some of his buddies with him to watch him clean my plow. He took a swing at me before I knew what was going on, and, if I hadn't been quick as a snake, that would have ended the fight right there. I saw the swing coming and slipped it with my shoulder, ducking my head at the same time and trying to drift away. Boxing is footwork above all. It's hard to knock out a fellow that's going away from the punch. Paddy had taught me plenty about fist fighting and also plain go-as-you-please scrapping.

The fellow wasn't expecting what I did then, which was to swing my body toward him and kick him in the side of his leg, right at the knee. When he went down, I was on him and slammed a scissors grip around his middle with my legs. He tried to punch me, but I had him from behind, and the best he could do was try to elbow me.

One of his buddies yelled—"That's not fair!"—and tried to pry me loose. I shot my fist up between his legs where it would do the most good, and he staggered away, howling.

Several of his buddies guffawed, and one of them said: "All's fair in love and war."

It wasn't either just then, but the fellow I had in my grip was having a lot of trouble breathing, and finally gasped: "Uncle!"

I let him up.

By then a small crowd had gathered. Someone said: "The kid can fight some, too."

I got out of there before a roving philanthropist decided to match me against the whole regiment in a go-as-you-please fight. If Fred Grant heard of the affair, he spared me from being his show horse again. I suspect Custer may have had a word with him about that, and, also, about his usual condition.

As Tom Custer said: "Grant is at least half 'how-come-you-so' all the time. I wonder where he gets it. If a snake bit him, it wouldn't phase him." Then he laughed and added: "The snake would probably get drunk."

Chapter Eight

The time was an historic era. You may say—"No kidding, which era wasn't?"—but some are more significant than others. This was the beginning of the end for the Plains Indians and, as a matter of fact, a time of change in Indian policy that put them all onto reservations, or killed or banished those who resisted. Grant had come into office sympathetic to the plight of the Indian and had enacted a new policy of humane Indian administration, or thought he had, by turning over the reservations to various churches to provide agents. I suppose he thought that would end the perennial graft in the Indian Bureau. Custer and other officers fought the crookedness, Custer without sufficient discretion, which brought about his downfall.

Custer's trouble started because Grant was a trusting soul and his old cronies had their hands out, which he didn't expect, nor did he think that religious Indian agents would dip their paws into the collection plate. He was dead wrong.

Grant's policy eventually hardened toward the Indians, and that was the reason we were out floundering around on an expedition in their inner sanctum. It's a wonder they didn't meet us in force. Grant was also hopeful, based on advice he'd received from men a lot smarter than he at economics, that if gold were discovered in the Black Hills in quantity, it would relieve the financial panic into which the country had fallen in 1873. And even if it didn't, the new land open for settlement would relieve pressure on impoverished Eastern communities by attracting settlers to the new land that would open for homesteading.

Unfortunately for Custer, he was sucked into that morass of major economic woes and large-scale graft and ended up testifying before a Congressional committee hostile to the Grant Administration and, worse yet, gave testimony that infuriated President Grant, since it implicated his family in the notorious sale of Army post traderships. The latter resulted in the disgrace and resignation of his Secretary of War and warm personal friend, General William Belknap and, worse yet, implicated Grant's brother Orville. Custer was no politician and would have been the first to admit it and, also, that his own big mouth had got him into deep trouble. But that is getting ahead of my story.

There wasn't yet so much as a ripple on that stream, and Custer was happy as a boy during our whole expedition. I stayed pretty close to him as much as I could, and as a result met my first hostile Indians. Get that word—hostile. Of course, they were hostile. But not without cause. Those who hadn't gone onto reservations ignored whites as long as they were allowed to. They were people on their native land where they'd been born and grown up. The Indians I was about to meet were Sioux who, at the time the U.S. established its independence almost a century before, had been lords of this land. They still were, but not for much longer.

The acknowledged leader of the splinter groups of the many tribes of Sioux who didn't intend to become plowboys was Sitting Bull. He was accepted by all of the Sioux sub-tribes as the principal chief of the hostiles, although he was really only chief of the Hunkpapa sub-tribe. But only he had the prestige to attract the huge camp of Indians that were to be Custer's downfall. They were known everywhere as Sitting Bull's Sioux until they licked the Army and got their nominal leader demoted by propaganda to a "medicine man". It seems the rationale behind his demotion was that Sitting Bull allegedly hadn't actively fought at the Little Big Horn. Well, if so, let's not forget that Grant didn't actively fight in any battle he was engaged in as a general. Never fired a shot in the whole war. Did that demote the Great White Father in Washington to a craven, which was what the press implied that Sitting Bull had been? Of course, the press took its cue from the Army that was smarting over having taken a monstrous, embarrassing shellacking. In any case, when he was a young warrior, Sitting Bull had made his mark as an outstanding fighter, with many "coups" which was the only way he could be accepted as the "Old Man Chief" years later.

Significantly I was on an expedition with many of those who were to be actively engaged and go down to ignominious defeat at the Little Big Horn. They would be my friends and would remain my friends, in some cases, until they died. Most of them were good men, good fighters in their day with impressive records in large engagements during the Civil War. The day Custer died, however, wasn't to be *their* day. It was Sitting Bull's day. As one of the Cheyenne women, Kate Big Head, who was at Custer's last fight, said to a writer: "Sitting Bull was the Old Man Chief." That said a lot. He was the big cheese, the sacred elder. I wish I had met him before the Indian Bureau and jealous rivals in his own tribe got rid of him.

The government's intention to publicize widely the attractions of the Black Hills and draw settlers can be seen in the number of newspapermen who had been invited to accompany Custer. I've already mentioned the Bismarck *Tribune*, but its circulation was limited. The St. Paul *Pioneer* was represented by Professor Aris B. Donaldson as a special correspondent, who was also the botanist for the expedition. The St. Paul *Press*, the rival newspaper there, also sent a correspondent who was probably more interested in scouting the country for the Northern Pacific Railroad than in writing dispatches. The Chicago *Inter-Ocean* sent a correspondent and so did the New York *World* and the New York *Tribune*. I have copies of all the articles written by the correspondents of these papers assembled to help me with the infallible recollections of an old man. They naturally had different objectives, and it's especially notable that the St. Paul papers were certainly not interested in stressing anything that might help Dakota economically. In fact, the front-page articles of the *Pioneer* were devoted to the investigation by the congregation of Henry Ward Beecher's Plymouth Church into the allegation that he'd had a nine-year affair with a member of his congregation.

In scouting through the old newspaper reports, a couple of things stand out that are confirmed by later events. The correspondent of the *Inter-Ocean* asked a Mr. John Goeway (assuming he was real rather than a straw man): "Do you think the government will grant permission to miners going there [the Black Hills]?" Goeway replied: "If the miners are satisfied that there is gold there, all the governments in the world will not stop them working it." This, at least, sounded like a fellow who'd been around the West.

Another Chicagoan, P. B. Weare—who later helped despoil the Indians in Alaska—told the *Inter-Ocean* reporter: "It's clear to see from the fact of an official expedition being sent out, that they [the government] are going to work to destroy the Indians' title to the Territory."

It took another year of superficial appearances, during which the Army maintained a showy policing of the routes to the Black Hills, to prove the truth of that. Many of those I met with the 7th were engaged in that sham.

There was little for me to do with Captain Ludlow's detachment, so he allowed me to roam around pretty much on my own.

I don't know if the Custer historians have fully covered the details of the expedition of 1874, but I've read almost everything that's come out on Custer, and I haven't seen much in print about it. Anyhow, I'm going to mention only the high spots and the important names. I'm not sure any of it has much significance, except the final confirmation that gold had been found, but we were well into our long trek before we got to the spot where gold was allegedly found "in the very grassroots". Don't mistake me, however, with the cynical remark "allegedly"; there was gold there. The questions that remain in my mind are: When and where was the gold discovered, and by whom? Deadwood, which is in the Black Hills, certainly confirms that rich deposits existed. Those discoveries contributed to the Hearst fortune, of which almost the whole world knows. There has never been a gold producer to match the Hearst's Homestake Mine at Lead, which is for all practical purposes a part of Deadwood.

Members of Custer's command traipsed all over the vicinity of Deadwood, especially me and Nate Knappen. But neither of us discovered any gold in the grassroots or anywhere else. He'd turned over his gold samples to the official prospectors.

I was particularly anxious not to make myself a further target of resentment among the enlisted men by appearing to be an officer's pet, but the junior officers of the 7th showed a remarkable interest in me after I won my foot race. They were probably more tickled at what I'd done to the Custer boys than to Benteen's crowd, to say nothing of punching some son-of-a-bitch in the nuts that was asking for it, which didn't hurt my stock, either. They were a rough, profane crowd. Incidentally, although the outward attempts to get even with me by friends of the "punchee", or he himself, were cut off by Paddy O'Toole, someone did hit me with a good-sized rock thrown from the dark one night. If it had hit me in the head, instead of the shoulder, it might have killed me. As it was, I was sore in that shoulder for the rest of the time out and a while after I got back to St. Paul. So I always had to carry with me the fear of being ambushed. As Knappen said: "If they'll try to kill you with a rock at night, they'll try to kill you from behind a rock in the daytime."

So I kept my eyes and ears open at all times and made it a point never to be out alone.

The first of the junior officers that offered me an opportunity to get better acquainted with them was Lieutenant E.S. Godfrey. He was assigned as Captain Ludlow's assistant, but there wasn't much to assist with. I'd been introduced to him and worked around him for a few days, but he never made any special attempt to be friendly. Then one day, *after* I became famous, he must have decided to ride beside me and find out a little of my background.

As openers, he said: "That horse seems to like you pretty well."

He was grinning, and I knew that he was aware of Buns' record.

"Wanna try him out?" I asked.

"This one suits me just fine," he said. "I heard yours is sort of a one-man horse."

I thought a "no-man" horse was more like it, and mentioned it.

He laughed. "Damn' if that isn't so." Then he changed the subject. "Where do you hail from?"

I filled him in on my background, as much as I cared to let out.

"An orphan, eh? How old are you."

"I reckon about fourteen goin' on fifteen."

"You ought to go to West Point," he said. "General Terry could get you an appointment, I'll bet."

At least by then I didn't have to ask what West Point was.

He and I were riding with the flank escort at the time and were interrupted by something we frequently heard in that country, the buzzing of a rattler. Our horses both shied.

Godfrey turned to the trooper behind us and pointed. The man dismounted and turned his horse over to the trooper next to him and found a good-size rock to kill the snake with. It took him several attempts, but he finally smashed its head.

"Nasty things," Godfrey said. "They always give me the creeps."

"Me, too," I said. "We had a lot of them out there in western Wisconsin."

"I have bad dreams about the little bastards crawling into my blankets with me at night."

I think everyone did. But it's a funny thing. With the country crawling with them, the only thing I recall that got bit on that whole trip was a horse, and the vet saved it. If rattlers were looking for us, they sure wouldn't have much trouble finding us, especially at night. The fact is they want even less to do with us, or with big critters that aren't on their bill of fare, than we do with them. I've watched them when I was out alone to see what they do, and, as soon as they knew I was around, they crawled away as fast as they could, or, if they didn't think they could get away, found something to hide under. When they don't have these opportunities, they rattle and assume their defensive coil and hope to warn people away. I'll bet a lot of people and animals have put a foot down right next to one that's securely hiding and thinks it's un-detected, and never got struck.

Godfrey told me he came from Ohio, had been in the Civil War a short while, then went to West Point. I never under-stood why West Pointers are so determined that, if anyone is going to amount to anything, they have to go to their trade school. If it came down to it, I think officers who came up through the ranks were a lot better fit to command compa-nies, since most of them had been sergeants and, even when it came to higher command later, experience taught them as much as any other officer could have. They simply hadn't mastered the art of balancing teacups.

Tom Custer wasn't a West Pointer. I often wonder how high he'd have gone in the Army if he'd lived. Most of the of-ficers who were not of the West Point elite were kept out of the schools intended to prepare officers for higher command, which I always thought was stupid.

I think the best officer among the company officers in the 7th was Captain French. He wasn't a West Pointer. My old friend, John Ryan, would have backed me on that. He should have known. He was French's first sergeant for years and fought under him at the Little Big Horn when French com-manded Company M.

French was a handsome fellow and the best shot in the whole regiment, with both rifle and pistol. During the Last Stand, he fought, practically single-handedly, the rear guard action that enabled Major Reno's battalion to escape to the bluffs where they were finally surrounded.

I think that Captain French must have won a considerable amount on my racing ability since, after that, he singled me out to talk to. It wasn't long before he decided I needed some shooting lessons. I wasn't too bad with a rifle, but had never shot a pistol in my life. One evening, French took me out a ways from camp and started my training. I can still hear his calm, musical voice giving me my initial instructions. He unloaded one of the two Smith & Wesson Schofield pistols he carried, and said: "You don't need ammunition to learn the most important things about shooting."

I can't imagine why the Army preferred the slow-reloading Colt over the Smith & Wesson, unless it was that the Colt .45 had greater hitting power. Or maybe it was the name. Cartridges were loaded awkwardly into the Colt through a loading gate in its right side behind the cylinder, one at a time, and unloaded the same way, with an ejection rod. I'm not going to go into details, but the Smith & Wesson swung open on a hinge below and in front of the cylinder so the back of the cylinder was entirely exposed, and threw out all six empty cartridges at once with an ejector mechanism, or, if you'd shot less than a cylinder full, you could quickly open the pistol part way and pick out and replace the spent rounds in a third of the time you could do it with a Colt side rod ejector. And, of course, you could reload equally quickly by comparison. By the same token I can't imagine why the Army abandoned the repeating Spencer Carbine that gave the U.S. Cavalry such a huge advantage over the Confederates during the war. Again the consideration may have been the modest hitting power compared to the .45-70 used in the Springfield. In any case, I think whatever rationale was involved was stupid. Had the Smith & Wesson and Spencer been taken into battle, along with about twice as much ammunition, I believe Custer's battalion would have survived with modest casualties had they forted up. Few people know what a real hail of lead is necessary to stop an attack such as the Indians were making.

French told me: "We are going to practice aiming and pulling the trigger with the gun empty. I always carry six empty shells in my pocket to put in the gun when we dry fire. They claim it's easier on the gun. Here, watch what I'm doing." He tossed the gun around in his hand like a magician. Next he broke open the gun and showed me how to pull up the release on top behind the cylinder, and then handed it to me.

"You do it. First push it shut and make sure it locks."

After we got through how the gun operated, he had me take it firmly in my hand, plant my feet, with legs spread, and sight at a white rock. I already knew how to aim a gun, and a pistol is no different than a rifle.

"Now," he said, "pull the hammer all the way back to full cock and squeeze the trigger gradually . . . just take up pressure on it until the hammer drops."

I did as he told me.

"Good," he said. "You didn't jerk the trigger. If you jerk it, you'll pull the pistol off the target. You want to squeeze it off every time just like that, and, doing it this way with nothing in it, you can see that the sights will be aimed on the target in the same place after the hammer drops."

He had me practice like that for a few minutes, then placed a round in the gun, saying: "There's only one round in the six chambers. You won't know when it's going to come up, unless it's the last one you try. The idea is to have you squeeze off just as though nothing is in the gun. If you flinch, thinking the gun is going to go off, you'll see that's what you've done and feel foolish. You soon get over flinching that way."

Sure enough, after about two good squeezed off dry shots without flinching, I thought the next one would surely go off and, anticipating it, flinched.

French laughed. "You've just seen one of the two reasons why people say 'you can't hit anything with a pistol', and they really believe it."

"What's the other one?" I asked.

"They jerk the trigger and the barrel is pulled down. When you flinch, it's to one side or the other or up. Try it again."

I did, concentrating like mad on squeezing slowly and smoothly, and the gun went off with the result that it hit the white rock dead center. I must have had a grin a mile wide on my face.

"Good, kid! You're going to be a natural."

I flinched a couple of more times, because I missed, but I also hit pretty regularly. After that we practiced every day. We must have burned up a thousand rounds of Captain French's personal ammunition.

"I don't know how I can repay you," I told him one day.

"Don't give it a second thought. I'm planning to match you against all the officers of the Seventh in a pistol contest when we get back to the fort."

"Are you kidding?"

"Well, I may have been, but, come to think of it, I think you'd outshoot the whole bunch of them right now."

He was probably right. Even Custer didn't practice with a pistol, although he had a reputation as a good shot. He may have been with a rifle.

French told me: "I offered to set up target instruction for the whole regiment, but Custer told me it would take too much ammunition. I told him I could improve their marksmanship with no ammunition at all, and he looked at me like I was crazy. So much for crack regiments." Knowing I was pretty tight with the Custers, he didn't say any more, such as: "If you ask me, this regiment isn't what it's cracked up to be." His company was, though.

I got the course from French in rifle shooting, too, including the kind of wing shooting that Buffalo Bill was famous for. Like everything else, there's a knack to it, but practice is the real secret. In a nutshell, however, if you want to shoot a man off a running horse in even the hardest position—which is running directly at a perpendicular angle to you—you come from behind, pass him with the sights until you get the lead you think you need for the range, and then keep moving your sights exactly that distance ahead of him, and squeeze off while keeping your lead. If the target is running toward you or away, it's a lot easier to hit, and from head-on is just like shooting at a bull's eye. It was a knack that was going to come in handy for me and my best friend a couple of years later.

I mentioned Captain French's one-man rear guard action at the Little Big Horn. French had a little help from Lieutenant Charles Varnum, who I also met on the Black Hills expedition for the first time. He was destined to be the last surviving officer of the big fight, and I used to see him fairly often until he died, up in San Francisco. While I'm at it, I might mention that Varnum almost had apoplexy over Reno's failure to organize a rear guard to cover the retreat, and got in Dutch with Reno over it. Alone he tried to rally a number of fleeing troopers, but they were in a blind panic by then. As he told me in later years: "You've got to keep them from running in the first place. Once they start, it's contagious, like a bunch of sheep."

Tom Custer introduced me to Varnum. They were pretty good friends and had a lot of the same steel in them. They shared those killer blue eyes that denoted the type of man that doesn't take shit off anyone.

Varnum grinned broadly, when Tom introduced us, and offered me a hand just like I was a man. "I saw you wax old Tom here and his brothers the other day. Won some money on you, too, in the big race. I'm glad to know you."

He really was, too. There wasn't any snootiness in him,

and he didn't give a fig that I was only a kid. As I said, they measured you for what you did, not what you should be expected to do by your station in life, or age. By their measure, I now know, I was a man, though I had a lot of bad times before I got it through my own head. Who doesn't? Especially if you're a kid dumped into a man's world too young. Or maybe there isn't such a thing as too young. The world gets from people what it asks for. Some kids, not out of diapers, are unruly if nothing is asked of them, but, as soon as they get the lash, they straighten up. Some horses are headstrong till they find the man that won't let them get away with it. Buns and I were still fighting that out at the time. I'm not sure to this day who trained who in our case, but I know I loved him, and, I'm sure, in his own way he loved me. He was the best horse I ever had.

On Custer's last campaign Varnum was to be the general's chief of Indian scouts, and I can assure you he wouldn't have been if Custer hadn't placed a high value on him. As a matter of fact, the year before, Custer had singled him out when they were up in Montana, guarding the Northern Pacific Railroad survey teams, and had a lively skirmish with a band of Sioux who ambushed them. After the fuss was over, Custer had exclaimed: "Varnum was the only one who stayed on his horse during the whole thing!"

I asked Varnum about that once, and he said: "Pure military science. I thought we were going to be overrun and wanted a head start."

I'm sure that wasn't true. He was extremely modest. It's most likely why he didn't make general in later years, like some of the other officers of the 7th did—Godfrey for one. You had to toot your own horn, or write, or something, and he did neither.

Another non-West Point officer of the 7th who I rate high

was Tom Weir. He had been with Custer in Texas right after the war and got a commission in the 7th from the day it was formed. I got to know him fairly well on the 1874 expedition because he was a fisherman. We fished together every chance we got, and Nate Knappen right along with us.

Weir was a little older than most of the other officers and had a tough war behind him. He'd gone through it in the 3rd Michigan Cavalry and once been a prisoner of war for a while. About that he said: "Being a prisoner of the Rebs was no picnic. They didn't have enough to feed their own troops, and we got what was left over." He laughed, expecting me to know that leftovers didn't exist. "I got caught by a Reb sergeant on the way to prison camp, stealing corn from their horses, and thought I was really in for it until he stole some, too. They weren't really bad fellows, and, if our politicians on both sides had had a lick of sense, we'd never have fought each other."

I had a meal or two with almost all of the officers of the 7th who were along with the Black Hills expedition, and rode alongside them, too. There wasn't a really bad apple in the lot except Benteen—and Reno who joined the regiment later. I have a recurring dream about them in which I am back there and somehow know which ones are going to be killed with Custer. It's pretty eerie riding along beside a man and seeing God reach down and say—"And you're one."—and touch him with a gentle finger, like in Michelangelo's painting on the ceiling in the Sistine Chapel, then move on to another and say: "And you're one. . . ." Almost two hundred of those in the Black Hills, officers and enlisted men, and a good many horses, ended up as bones on a hill in Montana two summers later.

To make a story that's already long enough just a little

longer, there were a number of well-known incidents of that tour due to newspapermen being along. For example, Captain Ludlow discovered a cave, or at least thoroughly investigated one that the scouts knew was there. It was named for him. We went through what became known as the Floral Valley. In the season when we were there, it's one of the prettiest little dells on the face of the earth. Someone stood in one spot and collected twenty-three different kinds of flowers. Custer's considerable flair for writing covered its beauties in his report. Custer and a couple of companies of cavalry, as escort, climbed a peak known as Inyan Kara, with me right along.

Custer also got his grizzly. It was the top trophy for a real hunter then—I guess it still is. Teddy Roosevelt had the same bug as Custer, and in a lot of ways they were alike; for one thing both had an inexhaustible enthusiasm to excel in everything considered manly. Or maybe I should say "he-manly". As for trophy hunting, I could never see it, but when Bloody Knife came in pell-mell one day and told Custer he had spotted the grizzly he wanted, Autie jumped up like he'd just got an electric shock. "Where?" he yelled, scrambling after his Remington sporting rifle. It carried a tremendous load of powder and lead. Burkman was already leading up Dandy at a trot.

Autie handed me the Remington and leaped on Dandy bareback, like a jumping-Jack, and reached for the rifle. His eyes were blazing and he was breathing heavily. This was a Custer I hadn't seen before, with the light of battle in his eyes. He scared me.

I got hold of Buns as fast as I could and followed the "circus rider gone crazy" the best I could. I was lucky to keep him and Bloody Knife in sight, since his favorite scout had a pretty fast pony, too. But Buns was a match for them, and I was only a few yards behind them when Bloody Knife signaled where to stop and dismount.

They had a quick confab in sign language, and the scout scrambled up the rise behind which he'd seen the bear. Custer was quivering like a hunting dog twisting to slip his collar while he waited Bloody Knife's signal that the bear was still there.

As I was watching this little drama, Spike Ludlow galloped up. Custer turned abruptly and gave us a sharp look that warned us to be quiet and stay the hell out of the way.

Finally the scout made a motion for Custer to join him, and I marveled at the speed with which Custer ran up that steep slope, taking huge strides in the loose soil while packing a ten-pound rifle. It made me wonder how I'd outrun him in our earlier foot race.

Bloody Knife was concealed from the bear by a spruce sapling on the crest. He motioned Custer up behind him, then pointed. Custer peeked over, then cautiously moved beside the Indian. All his impatience left him at the point of joining battle. He caught his breath, then he brought up the Remington, steady as a rock, aimed carefully, and fired. I didn't realize it then, but I'd seen that element in him at work that made him a great cavalry general. True, this was a less hazardous situation than a battlefield, but the life-threatening danger existed. Bringing down a grizzly is not child's play.

Custer threw his hat in the air and did a war dance, whooping like a kid, but Bloody Knife didn't look happy yet. He'd seen too many bears knocked down only to get up and run, or charge and kill the incautious hunter. By the time we got up the hill, the scout had made clear to Custer that they should be damned careful about approaching the animal. Autie reloaded his rifle.

The bear lay a good hundred yards down the slope—a fair shot if it hit a vital spot. Bloody Knife worked up to some fifty feet from the bear and started pitching good-sized rocks at it. It didn't move. Cautiously he worked closer, eyed it from some ten feet away, and, when he was satisfied it wasn't breathing, went up, and kicked it. With another whoop, Custer rushed over and posed with his foot on the beast. It reminded me of the illustration in *Robinson Crusoe*, with Crusoe's foot on Friday's neck. I almost laughed. Good thing I didn't.

Nothing would do but that Illingworth be called to take a picture of the mighty hunter. I should have got in the picture with the bear, Custer, Bloody Knife, and Ludlow. I'd have been famous, but actually I pitied the bear. It must have started out the day with the same joy of life that humans do. I'm not much of a hunter because I always feel that way when pulling the trigger on an innocent animal. Of course, I've hunted to survive in the wilds, but not otherwise, although I understand Custer's type.

What I was impressed by most, however, was my first hostile Indian. The scouts had rushed in and told Custer they'd found a Sioux village. Custer got the details straight before he decided to take any action, which was characteristic of him for all of his reputation for rashness.

We had begun to find Indian trails after we hit the Floral Valley, but had only seen the tracks of their ponies. I was riding beside Custer when we saw smoke ahead. We rode farther and came across several campfires still burning.

"Here are our Sioux," Custer said. "Probably saw us coming and got scared out. Why else would they leave fires burning? Too bad. Maybe we can find them and convince them we're not going to hurt them." He turned to Looie Agard, who had kept near him all the time, and said: "Take the Santee scouts and a white flag, and see if you can find some of them. Tell 'em we're peaceable."

Agard was a good man, well known to the Sioux, and fluent in the language. Custer valued him highly, and Agard thought he could get away with asking: "Where the hell do you suppose I can get a white flag in this outfit, gin'ral?"

Custer silently pulled a white handkerchief out of his breast pocket and handed it to him. Looie tied it on a stick, and, armed with that, he started off with his Santee scouts. The Santee were Sioux, but several of the Rees, including Bloody Knife, followed. The Rees and Sioux were notoriously hostile to one another, and even Bloody Knife, who was half Sioux, hated them. The Rees had been quickly daubing on war paint as soon as they heard there were Sioux in the vicinity.

Custer yelled after the departing scouts: "Hey, Agard, be sure those Rees don't decide to start a war!" He then thought he'd better keep an eye on them himself and spurred after, discovering another small camp down the valley.

Some of the Sioux, including most of the kids, ran into the brush as Custer himself rode up. He wore his blue pants with the yellow cavalry stripe down the leg, although he had on a buckskin jacket. Some women ran while others must have been too scared to run. Their fear tells you something of what they'd learned about soldiers in their short lives. The men were mostly out hunting, but one of the men, Slow Bull, came out of the timber, probably to protect the women and kids as best he could under the circumstances.

Custer had the touch for dealing with Indians if he could get near them and start negotiating. His unfailing tactic was to smoke with them and feed them a lot. He and Agard and Lieutenant James Calhoun, whose company Custer had had brought up to make sure the Rees stayed in line, sat in a council circle, smoking.

I was more interested in circulating around and didn't see where I'd be in any danger, under the circumstances. It was a clean camp by Indian standards, with five big teepees. The women and kids, who had run off, came back as soon as they figured we weren't going to hurt anyone. I noticed one fairly good-looking Indian woman and found out she was Slow Bull's wife and the daughter of the famous Red Cloud. I wished I had something to give to the kids, who seemed more curious than afraid after they got used to us being there. They were a bright-eyed little bunch, just as curious as any kids, and willing to be friendly. Because I had nothing else, I gave them each a .45-70 cartridge, which caused them to babble among themselves and compare their cartridges.

After the confab had gone on for a while, the rest of the men came back, including One Stab who was the head cheese. Custer told them all: "I come in peace to see the country. If you will give me guides, I will give you lots of food and presents. I come from the Great White Father who wants to know more about the country of his children."

Can't you just hear the Indians thinking and probably saying to one another later and laughing—"*Children,* my ass!"—just as we would over somebody like Hitler saying he was our Great Father and we his *"children"*?

Custer did get four of the Sioux to come to our camp, but they weren't there for the reason he had hoped. They were a smoke screen for the camp to break and run, which it did. Can you blame them? The Rees had practically been sharpening their knives in plain sight.

While Custer was trying to get up some rations with which to load down the Sioux, the four started to slip away. Custer said to Agard: "Tell them to stay. We aren't going to hurt them. I'll send guards to make sure the Rees keep their hands off them."

He'd already had Bloody Knife pass along the word to the Rees, of whom he was the nominal chief, that he would run them all out of camp and never give them coffee or sugar again if they started trouble. But the four Sioux kept going anyhow, and Custer sent a big party of Santee scouts to bring them back, by force if necessary. You can imagine how that worked out. One of the Santees took hold of Long Bear's bridle, who tried to grab the Santee's gun, and shooting started. Long Bear cut out on his horse, but was probably wounded by a shot fired after him, since we found his bloody saddle and blanket the next day. Talk about trying to "kill them with kindness". One Stab was brought back without harm, and he stayed with us a few days as a guide, since he had no choice. Custer finally let him go during the night so the Rees wouldn't follow him and do him up. When the Rees found out about that, there was a real howl. But they minded what Custer said and didn't try to take up the trail. Custer was big medicine with them, and even more so were the sugar and coffee rations with which he supplied them.

These reservation Sioux in small bands, such as we met, were called "summer roamers", and I'm sure there were thousands of them farther west, hunting with Sitting Bull and other non-reservation bands in 1874. I have always wondered why, in the campaign of 1876, the Army didn't anticipate the presence of this transient warrior strength that was just as hostile when it could get away with it as any. These roaming bands were what tipped the balance and got Crook soundly thrashed and Custer killed. Sheridan hadn't overlooked their kind among the Comanches, Kiowas, and allied tribes in his campaign on the Southern Plains that very year of 1874, and he had seen that they were cooped up on the reservations so they couldn't join the wild bands. It was a key strategy in defeating the Southern tribes and putting them permanently on reservations. After looking into possible causes, I discovered that Sheridan, whose responsibility it would have been to put them on reservations, had his attention focused on race unrest in New Orleans in 1876. I am baffled to understand why all the "historians" seem to have missed that. When Sheridan finally became aware of what was happening, he closed the door too late at the battle of Warbonnet Creek.

Finally, before we started back, I went along with Custer and two companies of cavalry that escorted Charlie Reynolds on his way to Fort Laramie with the preliminary report of our scout, including the news that gold had been discovered. Updates of that news were often in the headlines for the next three years, at least.

Then we started home.

Autie, ever a showman, arranged our return in typical Custer style. He moved our whole train over to the Heart River and formed it in parade-ground formation. The wagons were lined up in four columns abreast, with the troopers in the positions of march they'd held throughout our travels. The band was in position to lead the whole shebang into Fort Lincoln blaring "Garry Owen" with all the pomp and ceremony of a British changing of the guard.

Illingworth took a few pictures of the preparations with the wagons in column. I can pick out Autie, in front of one of the columns with a magnifying glass, because he wore buckskins. And I can pick me out because I wasn't too far away from him. Tom Custer was next to me. I just had the picture out, and it brought back the sound of the band trooping us into Fort Lincoln.

Chapter Nine

Libbie Custer gave me a big good bye hug and kissed my cheek as I left. All the way back to St. Paul I could still feel her warm, soft lips, and considered never washing that cheek again.

She had whispered in my ear: "You're good for Autie. He always wanted a boy of his own, but I guess God didn't make me right to give him one." As we drew apart, I was surprised to see a mistiness in her eyes. I knew then that she really meant what she said. But why do women always take the blame?

Autie was watching and interrupted with: "Hey! Whispered secrets yet! What have I been missing here? He's getting too big to trust!" He was probably recalling himself at the same age.

He punched my shoulder playfully and took my hand and shook it a long while, holding my eyes with those bright blue ones of his shining in a way they only did around family and close friends. There was no hint of Boy General in them, only of boy.

Maybe he was just being droll, and maybe he recalled our buck-naked foot race. I didn't stand short on the Custer boys in the male department, even at fifteen. But I never had a single one of the kind of thoughts about Libbie that growing boys harbor—to me it would have been like desecrating a shrine.

Custer's last words to me were: "Give my best to General Terry and tell him to come visit us . . . and to be sure to bring you along."

They were on the porch of their quarters, waving, when I looked back, and they waved a long while after we pulled away in Ludlow's ambulance. I waved back and kept waving, thinking: *What a hell of a fine bunch of people the Custers all are.* I'd have bet a million they wouldn't have sent me to cotillion.

I wished the other Custer boys had been there to say good bye, but Tom was off with his company on a patrol somewhere already, and Bos had gone with him.

It seems to me that General Terry was awfully interested in my opinion of the 7th and its officers. I wondered why he simply didn't ask Ludlow. It's easy enough for me to figure out today: He had obviously heard that the Custers practically took me into the family and it was Autie that he wanted to hear about, but he thought he had to be indirect about inquiring. There must have been some jealousy there, despite Terry still being a general while Custer had been reduced to lieutenant colonel. If you'd mentioned the name General Terry to anyone back East, even a newspaperman, they'd have said: "Who's he?" But everyone knew the name Custer. Terry knew that if postwar rank had been determined based on fighting ability and war record, it should have been Custer who still wore stars, instead of the other way around. And almost everyone in the Army knew that Custer was General Sheridan's fair-haired boy.

After my return, Terry's first chance to get me where he could talk confidentially was up in my bailiwick in the carriage house. They'd furnished the place for me to include a couple of comfortable chairs, and he sank into one and got a cigar going. He didn't offer me one, probably because he thought I was too young.

"Well, young man," he started, after blowing a big cloud

of smoke upward, "I understand the Boy General took a shine to you. What do you think of him?"

The question surprised and embarrassed me. The slight sarcastic inflection he put on "Boy General" warned even a green kid like me that I had to be careful. I managed what sounds to me, even today, like a masterpiece of evasive tactfulness, Lord knows how.

"I like all of the Custers. They made me feel right at home."

Terry certainly realized there was a good chance that the Custers were buttering me up solely because of my connection with him. He never did grasp the genuine nature of our mutual affection, regardless of why it may have started.

"I hear they even found room for you in their quarters."

I wonder how he would have taken it if I said: "Yeah, but they never offered to send me to cotillion." I imagine I'd have been out on the street pretty quick if I'd said that. Of course, such a thought never entered my mind then. But, as an old coot, some devilishly wicked thoughts are always crossing my mind. I could even have mentioned that I shared the room with the two younger Custer brothers and Tom's rattlesnakes. Speaking of Terry and devilish thoughts, I have seen enough of the world by now not to have to wonder any longer why Terry and Sergeant Clery took such a shine to a promising young fellow.

"Custer has some fine horses," Terry said, changing the subject. "Did he let you ride any of them?"

"No, sir, but his brother Tom let me use a horse all the while I was there."

"So I heard." He laughed for the first time. "I understand you gave Tom quite a surprise with his *trick* horse."

I grinned, remembering. "I gave myself quite a surprise, too."

"How's that?"

101

"I was able to stay on him."

I could read pride in his eyes. Of course, he'd heard all about it and wanted to know how I felt about it.

"You cut a fine figure all the way around, Tom. I heard you gave the whole regiment a little lesson in foot racing, too. I used to be quite a runner myself when I was young."

He had the long, gangly figure for it, but he was beginning to get a little paunchy, and I'd noticed, whenever he put his arm around me, that he had no muscles. He'd probably also heard about the fancy work when I punched that son-of-a-bitch in the nuts. He'd had plenty of chance to talk to Ludlow, and even Fred Grant who'd come back with us on the train. Grant seemed to like me about as well as the Custers did. It's a wonder he didn't take me on a tour of the St. Paul whorehouses as a special favor. In the two weeks he stayed in town, he was famous down along the waterfront, and not because of his old man.

From the next question Terry asked me, I'd bet Grant had given a glowing report of my escapades.

"What do you think of the President's son?"

I missed another good chance to get tossed out into the street. I could have said what almost everyone knew, with the possible exception of Terry: "He's really a popular fellow, especially in the joints down along the river." As a matter of fact he'd stayed pretty well oiled all the way back on the train. Maybe he'd been drinking up his surplus before he got back to Chicago where Sheridan could put a dent in it. Or, if he was going home for a visit at the White House, before his old man drained it. Like I said, I get a lot of devilish thoughts as an old coot.

I said: "Colonel Grant was really good to me. I like him a lot." I might have added that his gambling penchant had put over a hundred dollars in my pocket. But I wasn't about to let that out. Terry would have insisted I put it in a bank account to draw interest.

Terry edged into his next question and asked: "Where did you eat when you were at the Custers'?"

I thought nothing of telling him the straight truth. "Why, with all the rest of them."

His pained expression alerted me that I might have put my foot in my mouth.

"But you had no suitable clothes," Terry almost gasped.

"Suitable clothes?" I asked stupidly.

"Never mind," he said, and turned to a lot of questions about the expedition in general before he got to something else that seemed to have been bothering him. (The next week the Terrys gave me my first suit of clothes. They were almost new, but someone's cast-offs, nonetheless.)

"Were you there when they found the gold?" Terry asked next.

What a chance to say: "Hell, yes! Did you know it was actually in Lounsberry's office in Bismarck?"

What I said was: "Yes, Nate Knappen and I both hung out a lot with the prospectors. We were right there when they made their first strike. Knappen works for the Bismarck newspaper." I suppose I really didn't have to tell him that, since all the correspondent's articles had been published.

"Where was the gold strike?"

"I don't know exactly, but it was right in the middle of the Black Hills. After the discovery, I rode out, for two days, with General Custer when he took two companies of cavalry and escorted one of his scouts . . . Charlie Reynolds . . . on his way to Fort Laramie with the news."

"I know Reynolds," Terry said. "A good man." Then he changed the subject again, saying: "I hope you watched how General Custer manages a wagon train. He's one of the best."

"I even got to drive a wagon most of one day. The wagon master took a liking to me, I guess, and said . . . 'Why don't you try your hand at it?' . . . and he showed me how to handle the team. He said I was so good, he'd hire me, but he was probably just being nice."

Little did I know. The wagon master, Mike Smith, would actually give me a job in a little over a year after I ran off from cotillion like Huck Finn. By then I was a long ways west of St. Paul, out in Montana.

My schooling was about to take up in earnest, which was another of the reasons Terry was interviewing me, maybe the main one.

He got to that subject and said: "Captain Ludlow says you're a natural at mathematics and want to be an engineer. I think that's a fine idea. In fact, maybe you can go to West Point in another year or so. It's the finest engineering school in the country." (If that was so, it didn't speak too well for the state of engineering in those days.) "Meanwhile, the captain says he'll start teaching you on the job, and I've arranged for you to go to Professor Randall's Academy. He's a well-known mathematician and engineer, and works on the side for the railroads."

"Yes, sir," was the best I could manage. "I think I'd like that."

That was the beginning of my long trek into railroading, and, as I said, I owe the Terrys a lot, if you rate money as the measure of success. Eventually railroad building made me a lot of money, but it didn't come like leaves falling off trees.

The pressure was on me every day from the Terrys, and even Ludlow, to go after a West Point appointment. I'd heard enough about it and knew myself well enough to realize I just wasn't cut out for it. I didn't want to be impolite about it, but it got on my nanny.

Worse yet, the Terry girls had started showing me which fork to use at the table, which I wouldn't have minded if we were actually eating, but they had set up a training table. Add to that their urging me to shine my shoes every day and go to church on Sunday.

Over the months, I got to thinking more and more about the fortunes to be made in the gold fields. Deadwood was just getting started, but I'd seen enough of wild Indians out that way to suit me a lifetime. The fields up in Montana were the ones that interested me. So I made up my mind to "cut and run". It wasn't easy. By then I'd got so I sort of liked the Aunt Polly routine better than Huck Finn had, especially eating regularly, and I had a few friends I made in school and on the job that I'd miss. So, despite my background as a kid on my own, it was still hard to break away. The only one I confided in was Paddy O'Toole.

He wasn't long on giving anyone advice, not even a kid that needed it pretty bad. When I told him I was cutting out, he gave me a long look, probing my eyes until I looked away. His look had about all the advice I needed. All he said was: "You know what the hell you want to do. Do it."

I'd made another really unusual friend during my year back in St. Paul, considering our different backgrounds, but we had one thing in common. We both loved General Custer. He was Tom Rosser, who'd been Custer's roommate at West Point. Their friendship survived fighting each other on opposite sides in the war.

In 1873 Custer had provided a military escort through Sioux country for Rosser and his surveying crews for the Great Northern Railroad. Tom was chief engineer for the expanding railroad, which intended to cross the continent through the northern tier of states and territories. General David Stanley was the nominal commander of the escort troops, but it was Custer who had done the only fighting. In one of the skirmishes Custer had marveled that Varnum had stayed in the saddle during the whole fight. I'll tell you later what the Indians thought about that skirmish that came across in the official reports like a great Army victory.

General Rosser showed up on the train I was taking West, having finally cut out. I had added to my wad of a hundred bucks earned racing in 1874, and felt pretty well fixed, having been able to buy my own ticket. Nonetheless, I was alone and I'd have liked to have a sidekick with me. I'd written Nate Knappen and invited him along, but only got an enigmatic letter back, the substance of which was: **I don't think I'll stick my head out of my hole just now. Especially around Bismarck. I know too much.** I had an idea what he knew too much about and realized that I knew as much and had better keep quiet about it. If the truth leaked out about the alternate plan to plant gold samples, if necessary, the bad publicity would have shut off money, especially from Congress, which was all too conscious of what the newspapers reported. Millions of dollars rode on development of the Sioux country, and some determined men who, being behind the various projects, a few of which were only schemes at that time, would have balked at anything. One of the projects was to be the Great Northern Railroad for which I'd be working in a few more years. The big men weren't above having someone disappear, if it looked like they were in the way. Knappen, in particular, could have told what he knew, which would have resulted in a lot of bad publicity for Grant's beleaguered administration, already under attack even from his own party for massive corruption.

I didn't see General Rosser come into the car, and by then he was hard to miss, having put on about a hundred pounds over what a first-rate cavalryman would like to carry. He came from behind and sat down beside me with a sigh, saying: "Hi, kid, where are you headed all by yourself?"

I told him my sad story. He took it about like Paddy O'Toole had. "You're gettin' to be a man now," he said. "Go it." Then he laughed, and what a great laugh he had, a great— "Haw! Haw!"—rumbling up out of his broad chest, and he squeezed my leg, as he laughed, with a big paw. Somehow it didn't remind me of Terry's grip. Here was a fellow with a great hand for wielding a saber.

"So yer headed out to see Fanny." Terry would have died before he called a general Fanny, even if it was Custer's West Point nickname. "Well, he ain't home just now. Back in Noo Yawk hobnobbin' with the high and mighty." I must have looked blank, because he added: "He knows a lot of rich dudes like James Gordon Bennett, who also happens to own a newspaper. And he likes to pal around with actors." He guffawed. "Shakespearean actors at that, like Lawrence Barrett."

Oddly enough, by then I knew what a Shakespearian actor was.

Rosser snorted. "Jesus Christ! Hamlet!"

He pulled a flask out of an inside coat pocket and offered me a pull, which I turned down. In those days the taste of liquor made me sick. He took a big swig and wiped his mouth, capped it carefully, and put it away. "You know who I'd like to see play the melancholy Dane?"

I shook my head. I even knew who the melancholy Dane was since Professor Randall figured some of his better students ought to get a classical education, and he made us read a lot of books.

107

"Buffalo Bill." He snorted. "I can see him in a doublet and pair o' them tights, like a trapeze artist."

I laughed along with him. From his description I got a graphic impression and I've never seen Hamlet played without thinking about it. Buffalo Bill Cody was getting a national reputation from the blood and thunder stories of Ned Buntline and his traveling play called "Scouts of the Plains", starring Buffalo Bill. Buntline had even talked Wild Bill Hickok into touring with it for a while, till he got tanked up and shot up the fake Indians. He had probably needed the money.

With that in mind, I suggested: "Or Wild Bill Hickok, maybe."

"Him, too," Rosser agreed, brightening up even more. "Them fancy pants dudes Fanny toots around with will only get *his type* in trouble, and I told him as much."

How true that turned out to be. I wish I'd asked Rosser what "type" he had meant Custer was. He'd probably have said: "A wild man." Like that circus rider gone crazy with more gold braid than a French admiral.

Rosser corked off to sleep, sitting up, and soon slumped over against me, snoring. I thought: *A cavalryman can sleep anywhere. Even on a moving horse*—as I'd discovered how to do for myself.

I didn't mind. I slumped back against him and we had a good nap together. I wondered why he hadn't brought a private palace car along, and found out he'd been in too big a hurry. By then all the railroads had a few, for the big bugs. Everyone loved them, especially the dining facilities.

At Bismarck, Rosser had some business to conduct with Clement Lounsberry, and invited me along. "I'm goin' over to the fort later," he said. "There isn't a fit place to sleep in town, and the best one is full of pants rabbits." It was the common military name for cooties, the familiar lice that even generals had to suffer in the field.

I politely begged off and headed over to the fort alone. For some reason I thought it might not be a good idea to notify Lounsberry that I'd be wandering around on my own.

At the Custers' quarters, I found Tom the only Custer home, along with John Burkman and the black cook. Tom lived high when Autie was gone. It was probably the only time that liquor ever flowed in Custer's quarters at Fort Lincoln.

Tom welcomed me like a long lost brother. I hoped he didn't have some new snakes to show me.

"C'mon in, keed! Long time no see." He grabbed me and gave me a Custer bear hug and dance. "I suppose you've come to steal my horse."

It hadn't occurred to me, but it seemed like a good idea after thinking about it.

"How is Buns?" I said.

"Fat and saucy. Hasn't thrown anybody since late yesterday afternoon. Want to take him out for a turn?" It sounded like a dare that might be calculated to see if I'd lost my guts from living a year back with the dudes.

"Why not?"

So that was my first order of business. Buns seemed to remember me, like a good horse does with someone they respect. It didn't keep him from trying to throw me, though. I used that spade bit bridle and checked damned close for a curb strap before I got on him. He took his first hop before I straddled him, but I hung on through a few corkscrews, and finally got my foot in the other stirrup just as we took the fence. It took about a five mile circuit at a flat run to take a little of the steam out of him.

When we slowed down, I was breathing hard but had loved every minute of it. I said to him: "Well, how did that grab you, you rip-snortin' son-of-a-bitch?"

If horses could talk, and some like Buns almost can, I'd bet he'd have said: "Right smart!" By then so many had called Buns a son-of-a-bitch, mostly after they picked themselves up out of the cactus, he may have thought that "son-of-a-bitch" was his name. We loped back as sedate as a lady riding in the park—well, almost, except when he decided to shy about ten feet sideways, like a flash, every so often. I felt like I was home.

That night after a dinner shared by Tom Custer, Tom Rosser, and Tom Ballard, where I had my first glass of wine ever, I also got some of the best advice I ever got about a military career.

It didn't include advice to go to West Point. Rosser said of that: "You'll get the same result drinking beer and butting your head against a wall every once in a while. I never would have gone except that in those days a poor kid couldn't get what passed as an education any other way." He looked over at Tom Custer with slightly unfocused eyes and said: "I'd like to have seen you at the Point."

"Not my idea of schooling," Custer said. "Too much bullshit! I'd have lasted about a week."

Rosser said: "More like two or three days. I never understood how Fanny stuck the course."

"He's sneakier than I am."

"He never struck me as sneaky, but he's got that unsuspected side to him. He can bottle a lot up, if he wants to. He wanted to be a general. The only way he knew to get there was to finish West Point."

By then I was feeling the wine and put in: "Boy General."

That got me a couple of pretty sharp looks. They hardly expected that from me. In fact, it's hard to figure what they expected of me.

"He'd never have made boy general or any other kind, it if it wasn't for the wah," Rosser mused. "Me, either."

Tom Custer said: "If you ask me West Point ruined Autie."

Rosser looked surprised. "What the hell do you mean? It was the makin' of him."

"Naw," Tom disagreed. "It made him too damn' tame and conservative."

I never found out if he was kidding or not, because he passed out in his chair and then fell on the carpet.

Rosser bent over him and looked at him cock-eyed. "Here, kid," he said. "Help me straighten him out so he doesn't wake up stiff and sore."

After I did that, Rosser took a pillow off a chair and passed out beside Tom. I went up to bed. They were still there snoring peacefully, side-by-side, when I got up in the morning.

Those were my last memories of what you might call civilization. I went up the river on a steamer the next day, bound for Fort Benton. Tom Custer wanted me to hang around, but I hadn't told General Terry I was leaving and I wouldn't have put it past the good general to have me brought back in irons "for my own good" since what I was doing would strike him as insanity.

The two Toms went to the boat with me, Custer to see me off, and Rosser because he was headed for Montana on the same boat. As a result of such distinguished company, I met another individual who would have a prominent rôle in Custer's Last Stand, Grant Marsh, the captain of our boat, *the Far West*, who was already a legend in that country.

On parting, Tom Custer shook my hand and held on for a long while. He said: "If you ever lose your mind and decide to get into the Army, for Cris' sakes don't enlist. Autie can get you a commission in the Seventh. And, whatever you do, never even think of going to West Point!"

I never did, not because I thought it didn't have its good side, but because I knew I wasn't cut out for it. I didn't want to be a boy general, or any other kind. I had the poor-boy complex and wanted to salt away enough money so I'd never be hungry or in want again, and I didn't like the idea of getting it through charity, which I considered accepting the Terrys' help to be. Even being an officer in the Army didn't appeal to me. Most of them were peeling the potatoes pretty thin all the time and had to borrow money to get by unless they had outside incomes. Few did.

Chapter Ten

Fort Benton, my destination in Montana Territory, was the head of navigation on the Missouri River. That is, it was the head of navigation when there was enough water in the river to make it, which was from the time the ice went out until early summer, a period during which snow melt from the mountains kept the water high. At other times the river was navigated by the crude buffalo hide coracles, known as bullboats, or, on the winter ice, by sleds pulled by manpower.

The water was still high enough to make it to Fort Benton and we got there in record time, according to Captain Marsh. I don't recall what that time was, but it was several days. We passed a number of other boats returning, and stopped to help pull one off a sandbar. Bullboats were floating down the river, carrying busted miners and anyone else who couldn't afford steamboat fare. Sometimes old-time trappers and ad- venturers did it simply as a ritual, even it they could afford boat fare. It was what you did, a habit of over a half century, when returning to civilization to market goods, get drunk and disorderly, try out the new crop of whores in St. Louis, and come back up the river before freeze-up to start another round of the same.

The peak of the fur trade was long past, but it got into the blood. Some trappers and hunters hung on because they were putting off going home to die on the old family farm, smelling of pig shit, but they knew that someday they'd have to—even the most famous of them, Jim Bridger, had gone back to a Missouri farm by then.

Along the banks of the river were the camps of wood-cutters, since the steamboats all depended upon wood to fire their boilers. The camps were crude and the life was hazardous beyond the average, since they were in the middle of Sioux country, but I never heard that the casualty rate was high, because, I suppose, a lot of them were married to Indian wives—a breed known as "squawmen". They undoubtedly filled their Sioux relatives with plenty of grub, but I wouldn't have risked it for all the tea in China.

Besides, in summer, the river was infested with mosquitoes. Speaking of mosquitoes, Marsh traveled day and night, when there was enough light to see, but, on dark nights, he tied up and anchored in midstream, in the widest spot he could find, where there was a fighting chance that some of the mosquitoes wouldn't come out to eat us alive. By then, of course, mosquito bars were known, a netting developed by the British in India, and, as a matter of fact, my pal, Nate Knappen, had done a good business with them as a sideline in Bismarck. I sure had one with me.

I didn't see too much of General Rosser on the trip, since he was a devotee of that old American gentleman's sport, poker, and there was a game going day and night in the main salon. Rosser was apparently pretty good with the pasteboards, since he looked happy every morning when I met him at breakfast before he headed for bed.

That's how I recall making it to Fort Benton the first time. I was to spend a lot of time up in that country, on and off, but none of it would prove as interesting and adventurous as that first year.

Fort Benton was a typical river port, not as big as St. Louis or Kansas City, but a dose of the same. It was the jumping-off place to supply the gold camps to the west, and the Diamond R Freighting Company had almost a monopoly. Wharves and warehouses showed a lot of activity when a new boat came in, an event that turned out cussing teamsters and roustabouts and straining horses, and, after unloading, everyone but the horses rounded to a saloon for a "smile" to rest up from their labors. A "smile", of course, was a drink.

Rosser collared me, saying: "You don't want to stay around here. You'd better come out to the fort with me. I've got some business out there and a lot of old friends."

I wondered if he didn't have another game as well, because I was sure that by then Terry was looking for his missing ward, and there were telegraph connections to both Fort Lincoln and Fort Benton.

Most of the old friends Rosser mentioned turned out to be West Pointers and were often former enemies who had reverted to old friends as soon as the shooting war was over. Foremost among those I was to meet was General John Gibbon, then a colonel, busted down like Custer to a less exalted rank than he held during the war. He was bucking to get back at least one star, and the sooner the better as he saw it. This certainly was one of the things that was to have a large impact on the happenings fated to follow the next year when the Army was dispatched on the final campaign to subdue the Sioux and Cheyennes and their peripheral allies, such as the Arapahoes. The Army hadn't yet discovered that their job was going to be somewhat like charging hell with squirt guns, especially with the limited men they were provided. If rival commanders had co-operated, they would have had a better chance, but they never did—far from it—as I was destined to learn first hand.

There was a telegraph line between Fort Benton and nearby Fort Shaw where Gibbon had the headquarters of the

7th Infantry of which he was the commander. He also commanded the mountain district of the Department of Dakota, which included Fort Ellis at Bozeman. The telegraph was what got Rosser an Army ambulance to carry us out to the fort where Gibbon himself met us.

Gibbon had a surprise for me. First, he shook my hand just as Custer had, which should have alerted me that he knew who I was. Of course, I was wearing my one good hand-me-down suit, but by then it was pretty rumpled and soiled and sure wouldn't have persuaded him I was a gentleman fit to have his hand shaken by a member of the elite.

After the two old friends got the—"Howdy Tom. Howdy John."—out of the way, along with my introduction, Gibbon speared me with the familiar Army officer look and said: "I've got a telegram over at my office about someone with your name."

My heart sunk. In those days on the sparsely settled frontier, the long arm of the commanding general of a department reached everywhere. Here I was, about to get tossed into irons and carted back to St. Paul as a mental case.

"Yes, sir?" I said, and it was a question.

I felt a little better when he grinned and winked at Rosser.

"It seems like General Terry has a personal interest in a fugitive going by your name. He said, if I was to run across Tom Ballard, to take care of the strong-headed young fellow and keep an eye on him until he comes to his senses."

I wondered which of the various people I considered trusted friends had given General Terry a tip about where I might be found. I ruled out Paddy O'Toole, though he was undoubtedly asked. I didn't rule out Tom Custer, though, or even Rosser. I never found out, but both of them had a motive to butter up Terry; in Tom's case for his brother's sake, not his own.

"I may have a job for you while I'm keeping an eye on you," Gibbon added. "I understand you've been working for Ludlow and have a grasp of surveying."

"Yes, sir," I said. This wasn't exactly what I had in mind, but it would conserve my savings while I looked around.

"You want a job?"

Rosser was watching me and I got the message from his nod that he thought it would be a wise idea to take whatever I was offered. When I was young, it never occurred to me to haggle in this kind of situation and ask: "What kind of job?" It wouldn't have been good policy anyhow. All those old-time officers, especially the ones who had been generals, weren't used to being democratic. They were lords of their domain and had been known to have people shot or hung out of hand with no consequences following from the courts.

"Yes, sir," I said again. I didn't care what kind of job it was, under the circumstances. I could always skip out if I wanted to. It's a good thing I didn't, or I'd have missed out on an early Christmas present that changed my whole life.

Gibbon said to Rosser: "Let's go over to my quarters and libate a little, Tom, and you can tell me what you've been doin' with yourself since the war."

Rosser said: "I took out a license to steal. It beat goin' back to the old cotton, corn, and sweet taters."

Gibbon guffawed. "That's why I stayed North, Tom."

It was Rosser's turn to guffaw—I didn't know why then, but I later found out Gibbon went to West Point from the South and stayed with the Union during the war rather than go home like a lot of loyal Southerners had.

Since I wasn't invited out of the gathering, I tagged along. And would you believe this? I was put up in the colonel's quarters along with Rosser, just like at the Custers. Only Gibbon didn't have a wife there. She was back East somewhere, as I recall—assuming he even had one—I can't remember.

I got a real earful, as I usually did, being the quiet little mouse in the presence of my *betters*. I might as well not have been there when the two got to talking. We ended up on the verandah of Gibbon's quarters after a lunch. Rosser offered Gibbon a cigar from a leather case.

"Thank you kindly," Gibbon said, smelling it appreciatively. "It's hard to get a good one like this up here, especially a fresh one. Lucky to get two-fers by the time winter is over." Two-fers were the malodorous two-for-five-cent cigars so popular with the poor.

"How do you like it in this god-forsaken country?" Rosser asked Gibbon.

"Not too bad. I never go out in the winter."

"How the hell do you manage that?"

"I delegate everything but delegation."

Rosser laughed. "I think you're gonna have yore little idyll busted up pretty soon."

"So I heard."

"Old Grant is tired of coddlin' Injuns," Rosser continued. "I was in Washington last fall and talked to him. Imagine that. What did you think of him? You were around him a lot."

"A helluva good general. A damn' poor President."

Rosser nodded. "Well, he's in a bind and knows it. He'd like a third term, but he knows he's not gonna get one with a money panic on. That's why he wants to open up the Black Hills. Custer found his gold there for him, and he wants to start pumping the yellow stuff into the country. Of course, he didn't figure that out all by himself."

Gibbon nodded, blowing cigar smoke high in the air. He pointed a finger at it and said: "That's where the Indians are going. We've heard rumbles about it already. Even our Crow

Indians have heard and can't wait to see the Sioux get it in the neck. I imagine I'll be right in the middle of it. The thing to do is come at them from all sides. A column from Nebraska up the old Bozeman Trail . . . Custer from Fort Lincoln . . . me from here."

And that was the way it turned out, and me right in the middle of it, too.

The talk turned to Rosser and his job as chief engineer of the Northern Pacific. He told Gibbon: "The gold can't turn on any too soon for me. I'm lucky to still be on the payroll. When things pick up, we'll push across the Missouri with a bridge at Bismarck and come across to the Yellowstone. Old Billings is champin' at the bit."

We finally got around to what my job would be. Gibbon said to me: "Since you know something about surveying, we can sure use you up here. I'm going to assign you to Lieutenant Bradley. I've got some jobs laid out right here at Fort Shaw to spend the money we've got for buildings before Sheridan decides to give it to somebody else."

"Suits me," I said.

"It'll pay thirty a month, and found. We'll call you an assistant. Nobody can argue about that." He laughed a little and I think it was because Terry had authorized that much to keep me out of trouble, suggesting that Gibbon find a title for what I did so some War Department inspector wouldn't question it later.

It's nice to have sponsors. I found one all my life, somehow. They call it "friends in high places". I have to laugh thinking about that. Up in that country I was destined to see some people with "friends in high places" who weren't exactly elated by it, since the "friends" got there on the end of ropes, and they suspected they were scheduled to be next in line. Plummer got his that way down in Alder Gulch a decade before, but plenty more were swung off later. And not always for what they did. As often as not it was for what the community was afraid they might do next.

The following day Gibbon took me over to headquarters and sent for Lieutenant James Bradley to tell him he had an assistant. Bradley saluted the colonel and waited respectfully to find out why he was there.

Gibbon said: "Jim, I've got you a surveyor to help lay out those new buildings."

Bradley looked me over then for the first time and shook my hand in a friendly fashion. He'd been around and knew my youth might actually be hiding a man inside. Brad was older than he looked, and had a tough Civil War behind him, including some time as a Reb prisoner, but it hadn't soured him on life.

He put me right to work, laying out corners for a new barracks. The old ones were falling down like most temporary construction was on all the forts that were hastily built on the frontier after the war. I liked working with him. He never said "Do this," or "Do that," but "What do you think about . . . ?" It made it seem like your own idea.

So I had a job and was wondering if I'd make enough to buy a horse. It turned out I wasn't going to have that worry.

I got a note from a freight agent at Fort Benton to come over and take charge of a shipment that was consigned to me. That was a real stumper. I wondered who the hell would be sending me freight. The freight had been sent by Tom Custer, and had a note with the bill of lading that said: **I could hardly wait till Christmas to send you your present, since the river will probably be frozen to the bottom. This is a present from me, Autie, and Libbie.**

The freight was Buns, a "condemned" McClellan saddle,

and his bridle with the spade bit. Condemned was an Army term for equipment that was judged unusable any longer. This saddle looked pretty new to me, and I wondered if condemned in this case didn't come closer to "misappropriated".

Buns had come up in a stall built on the boat's deck and, to keep him there, it had to be lined with some boilerplate they'd had on board, luckily, since he'd kicked his way out of the plank stall they had started him out in and had tried to jump into the river.

I could tell he was glad to see me because, as soon as I turned my back on him, he bit me. He hadn't changed a particle and tried to throw me as quick as he could when I got onto him. When he found out he was doomed to his usual bad luck at that, he took me for our customary run. When I finally got him turned around and came back, Sergeant Meagher, who'd accompanied me to pick up a few things for the fort, got off a masterpiece of understatement.

"That son-of-a-bitch is a real firecracker!"

Chapter Eleven

The country is always the overlooked character in stories, as a rule, despite being the one with the greatest impact on the action in a good many cases, especially if the living characters have been in the locale very long, since the land makes the man. The West sure as hell made me.

I was in Lewis and Clark country when I got to Fort Shaw. Lewis and Clark had both been Army officers and the first purely American explorers of the West. Naturally they had been the first to leave detailed records of the route from St. Louis to the Pacific, since that was what President Jefferson had dispatched them to do. They had spent a great deal of time in the area I was now in and had reported fully on it.

The main feature of the country that figures in my story was its rivers, which all run east, since the Continental Divide lies west of Fort Shaw. Two principal rivers are the Missouri and the Yellowstone, a tributary running into it from the southwest. The whole western side of Montana is mountainous and covered with coniferous growth, with wooded flatland along the rivers. The grass is good in most places, which was always something to consider in moving through a country, particularly for the Army with a large number of cavalry horses and supply wagons.

The valley of the Yellowstone was to be our theatre for the campaign of 1876 against the Sioux and Cheyennes. There were not over 15,000 white people in the whole of Montana Territory at that time. Think about that.

The main routes into western Montana—which was the only settled part so far as whites went except around Fort Union in the northeast—were via the Missouri River by steamboat to Fort Benton, or by the freight route north from the railroad in Utah. The Bozeman Trail had been a hopeful short cut, but its life was *cut short* by an Indian named Red Cloud. The Army had put three forts along the trail in 1866 to keep it open: Fort Reno, Fort Phil Kearney, and Fort C.F. Smith. The Sioux, under Red Cloud, made them too expensive to keep in operation, and they were shut down, along with the trail.

But while the Bozeman had been open, that country became pretty well known. The old Bozeman route would be the avenue by which the Army would send one of the columns after the Sioux the year after I got up there. So, as you can see, they would be operating in well-known geography, although unpopulated by whites. When the Custer "coverup" started, there were many who wanted to make that country out as an unexplored, howling wilderness. It had been thoroughly explored, even by the Army. If it hadn't, the scouts employed, both Indian and white, were thoroughly familiar with it.

In those days I had a strong urge to see more and more of the West, but it wasn't happening under the eye of Lieutenant Bradley. We were surveying plots of ground to expand the fort and not much more, and I was discovering my itchy foot that eventually picked a profession for me. Brad wasn't any happier than I, and would have preferred to be out exploring and map-making, but wasn't free to move on since he had a wife and children. I was.

Events helped me decide to do just that. After the first

night at Colonel Gibbon's, I'd been assigned a bunk in the barracks, and, although I knew how to get along with the troops for the most part, there was no way I could escape the "teacher's pet" label, since everyone on Army posts learned about everyone else sooner or later. I was rightly seen as the colonel's special charge, and the news circulated that was because I was connected well with General Terry. It all led to making me a pretty good bare-knuckle fighter. I hadn't lost the knack of a swift kick to the right spot, either. I never lost a one-on-one fight. None of that sat too well with the soreheads or, for that matter, even with the run of soldiers, and it was bound to lead to serious trouble for me sooner or later. It came sooner, and I was ganged one dark night and had the hell beat out of me.

When Lieutenant Bradley saw the head on me the next day, he was all for taking it to Colonel Gibbon and launching an investigation to make someone pay. I didn't see it that way, but couldn't talk him out of it. Before anything could come of that, I threw together my few belongings and headed out on Buns. I had no idea where I'd go, but thought Fort Benton might be a good starting place. I could always go back to St. Paul with my tail between my legs. Or even Fort Lincoln where I could probably get some kind of work through the Custers. But it would be the "teacher's pet" route all over if I did that. At least I had some money to coast on while I looked around. It's a wonder they didn't clean me out when they cleaned me up. In any case, my penniless days had pounded into me the wisdom of saving as much as I could of whatever money came my way. I had almost all of two months' pay, plus my original savings, still in my pocket. My natural and growing thriftiness also suggested that I get a job as soon as possible.

At Fort Benton I found a place to stay, but didn't need it

long. I was wandering around my first morning in town, looking the place over, when I felt a heavy hand on my shoulder. The thought flashed through my mind that Gibbon had sent a patrol after me. I spun around and was mighty relieved to see it was Mike Smith, who had been Custer's wagon master on the Black Hills campaign.

"Hello, kid," he said. "You're about the last person I expected to run into." As we shook hands, he stated: "C'mon in and join me for a smile. I forgot my toothbrush."

I was sure he was kidding. His kind didn't own toothbrushes. In fact, like the old song goes about "Old Grandad When The West Was Young", I'd bet he didn't even own a comb, and "combed his hair with a frying pan". At that time of day, pretty early, it was known as an "eye-opener". I read somewhere that Buffalo Bill introduced the Grand Duke of Russia to the custom when he came to the U.S. for a buffalo hunt, and the Duke pronounced it "more refreshing" than brushing his teeth.

That rough greeting was Smith in a nutshell. I was sure as hell glad to see him, and, although I didn't drink yet, I gladly joined him. I remembered that job offer he'd made the year before and intended to see if he had been serious about it.

At the bar, Smith eyed me and asked: "What's yer pizen?" He probably suspected I might not drink, but in those days a lot of kids my age not only chewed and smoked, like I did, but put away their share with the best of them.

I confessed: "I don't drink much. Can't get it down without choking on it."

"That's probably because the rotgut somebody gave you was cheap stuff." He said to the bartender: "Bring out the smoothest stuff you've got, Hank."

I noticed the bartender had to search around under the bar

125

before he finally brought out a bottle. "Best in the house," he said. "Straight Kentucky." He dusted off the bottle, so I knew he didn't very often have a call for expensive stuff.

Smith eyed the bottle, and nodded. "OK, pour two of those. I'll show you how to take it," he said to me. "First take it up and sniff it."

I did and was very conscious of Hank's watching to see how I made out. I sniffed it and it sure didn't smell like the stuff I'd smelled before.

"Now take just a little sip and roll it around in your mouth a while before you swallow it," Smith advised. "If you don't like it, get rid of it in the spittoon, and I'll finish the rest for you."

I swirled it around in my mouth and was surprised that I did like it. Smith was watching me closely and could read that on my face.

"OK," he said. "Now take a little more and do the same thing, then swallow it in a gulp."

I suppose I should have been surprised that a rough diamond like Smith was being so considerate, but appearances are deceiving. Like a lot of his kind, he had a heart of gold and wouldn't have hurt anyone that wasn't asking for it. I was learning from an old master. I did just as he said, and I didn't feel like puking as soon as it went down. It just had a nice, warm feeling. I tossed off the rest after swishing it around, and Smith smiled.

"Another one?"

"Not yet." Caution suggested I see how that one sat.

Smith downed his in one swig, then said: "Leave the bottle here, Hank. I'm trainin' you a new customer." He said to me: "Well, what the hell brings you out here?"

"I ran away from dancing school for one thing."

That raised his eyebrows. "Dancing school?"

"Yeah. Cotillion, to be exact."

"What the hell is cotillion?"

I told him.

"Jesus Christ!" he exploded. "No wonder Gibbon calls old Terry Daisy."

I couldn't have put it better myself.

"You'd better have another one," he suggested.

I was a little light-headed and feeling pretty good. Anyone who remembers their first drink of the real thing will know exactly what I mean.

He poured my second one without waiting for any response from me. "You can probably handle one more," he said. "Then we'll go tie on the feedbag."

I told him the rest of my story, and he didn't interrupt once, merely looking a little more interested over some parts of it.

When I finished, he said: "You're having quite a time. What do you aim to do now . . . head for the diggin's?"

"I sort of had that in mind when I first headed out here. I've *been* poor. I thought I might give rich a try, if I'm lucky."

He shook his head. "You'll have to be. Most of the big strikes are already filed up. How'd you like to take a job with me? You won't get rich, but you won't get any poorer, either."

I didn't have to think about that one long. "You got yourself a hand," I said. I hesitated saying "man", even though he treated me like one, just like everyone else but Terry had.

Smith took me up the street to a restaurant, and I imagine he was watching to see how I navigated. By then I was feeling for the ground with my feet, but I managed, and a big breakfast settled me back down.

127

"This is a great country," he said while we were putting away a buffalo steak and eggs, backed up by good bread and hot coffee with real cream and a lot of sugar. "You can make a pile hunting buffalo up here as soon as we wipe out the Sioux. They've been doin' it down south since they ran the Comanches onto reservations." This came out matter-of-factly. Everyone took it for granted that it was only a matter of time until the Sioux got theirs, and the sooner the better.

When we finished breakfast and were out on the boardwalk, he asked: "You got a horse and guns?"

"I got a good horse and my old Army Springfield."

He snorted. "It takes forever to get off a second shot with one of those. Illingworth took my picture with one for show, but I hope nobody thinks it was mine. It's as close as I want to come to one. I can't imagine why the Army gave up their repeating Spencers. You can buy one of those cheap. You got any money? And, come to think of it, you'll need a pistol, too."

He was wearing one in plain sight like most who came in from the trail, although the townsfolk didn't.

"I got enough, I guess. What do they cost?"

"You can get a Spencer and a good pistol for less than thirty bucks for sure."

"I can manage that."

He led the way down to a hardware that displayed a big sign: **GUNS AND AMMUNITION**.

The inside was a delight to anyone who liked guns, and I did. There must have been a hundred rifles and shotguns, gleaming, all in a row in a rack on the wall behind the glass display case that showed off dozens of pistols. The new Army style six-shooters were rare yet on the civilian market, but there were plenty of others that used metallic cartridges. Everyone in those days, who had the money, wanted to get rid of their slow-loading cap-and-ball revolvers. All the good gun-smiths were converting them to cartridges.

The clerk hovered over us, knowing who Smith was.

Smith pointed to a pistol, and the clerk took it out. Smith said: "This is a Remington cap-and-ball converted to Army ammunition. You can buy that cheap from any light-fingered soldier. You can even buy an Army Colt from deserters, but best not. The serial numbers will give you away, and the Army might take it back if you get around them. Try this." He passed the Remington to me.

After looking over a lot of guns, I left the store with the Remington and not a Spencer, but a Henry. It cost a lot more than an old Spencer, but I fell in love with it at first sight. It shot sixteen rounds of .44 caliber. The whole thing set me back sixty bucks, but the whiskey helped talk me into parting with that much. The storekeeper threw in a hundred rounds for the .44 Henry and a scabbard and cartridge belt for the pistol. I bought another hundred rounds of .45s for the Remington.

As we left, Smith said: "I reckon you feel like Wild Bill in that get-up."

I did, too. The feel of the heavy .45 strapped on my hip did something for me.

"I recall you know how to use them, too, thanks to old Tom French," Smith said. "And let me tell you something about that pistol. Never get it out and threaten anybody with it unless you're really willing to use it. Otherwise, you're apt to get killed for sure."

It was damned good advice. I never forgot it.

Smith was in town getting a train together to run one shipment of supplies to Fort Ellis and another shipment on down to the Crow Agency. I was outfitted to go with him,

provided he wanted me, and I already assumed he did. He
put me right on as what they called a swamper, which was
the assistant to a wagon driver. Smith drove a wagon himself
and was looking for a new swamper, since his had taken a
boat home, as he explained: "For no good reason. The son-
of-a-bitch wanted to go see his old mother . . . can you
imagine that?"

I could. I wished I still had mine to go see. It's possible
Smith didn't know who his had been. There was a common
old saying in the West about early pioneers in California that
just about fit the whole country:

> **The miners came in 'Forty-Nine,**
> **The whores in 'Fifty-One.**
> **They rolled upon the barroom floor,**
> **Then came the native son.**

Our route took us through Helena, known widely as Hell-
In-A-Handbag, but I didn't have a chance to take in the
sights. Smith pulled on through and camped ten miles
beyond it. He knew if he didn't, he'd lose a day while his men
recovered from a night in the saloons and girly dives. I was
too young to be tempted by that and, in fact, never did go for
that monkey business. Women and whiskey weren't to be my
weakness; money was. That's why I'm up here in a mansion,
not hurting for anything but the kind of good old company of
men who had the women and whiskey weaknesses in spades.
Whatever you say for them, every one was an individualist or
they wouldn't have been out in that raw country. You could
trust most of them with your life. And they didn't try to hide
their vices. I've always been wary of a man with no apparent
vices. My main one was smoking. I still enjoy a good cigar and
take a snort or two of whiskey every evening. There's no harm

in it taken in moderation. In fact, I think it helps me get a good night's sleep.

I stumbled into an unusual fellow at the Crow Reservation, a good friend of Mike Smith's. At first I took up with him simply because of my love of fishing. We were laying over a few days to rest the horses after we unloaded. It was a tough country on horses. The first night we were there Smith said: "You should come with me and see Tom LeForge. He came out here as little more than a kid and liked the Crows, and they took to him. Since then he's become almost a Crow himself. He's gone on their horse-stealing raids and war parties, and taken scalps just like them. Now he's a top warrior in their eyes . . . a *wolf*, which is what they call their best scouts and warriors. He can tell you more about this country and Indian ways than anyone you're ever apt to meet."

LeForge had a cabin and lived in that respect like a white, but was Indian in every other way. His Indian name was Horse Rider.

He looked me over pretty sharp without appearing to, when Smith introduced me, but he must have figured I was OK if I was with Smith. After getting to know him, I learned that he looked over every newcomer pretty closely.

Smith had grinned as he said: "Tom, this is Tom."

LeForge offered a big, callused paw that I could tell had a grip like a grizzly bear, though he wasn't one of those bullies who bear down in a handshake.

Smith added: "Actually the kid here is Tom-Two, or at least that's what the Custers call him so he doesn't get mixed up with the general's brother Tom. I guess maybe that'll do around here, too."

That got a grin from LeForge and got me another sharp look. I wondered why, and guessed because everyone knew

General Custer. What I didn't know then was that Tom LeForge thought Custer's reputation as an Indian fighter was a joke. I said earlier that none of the Army officers really knew beans about Indian fighting, and that was LeForge's opinion of Autie. I have to say I agree. The Army officers were mostly willing enough to fight them—with a few exceptions like Major Reno who enters the picture pretty soon—but never understood how to do it. You were safest if you made them come to you.

LeForge and Smith sat around the kitchen table, ignoring me, tossing down a few together, while we all smoked. Neither offered me the jug, but I had no desire to renew my recent acquaintance with booze after looking over the jug it was coming out of. It looked like the ones I was familiar with that had held the "pizen" that had gagged me in the past.

LeForge's Crow wife, Cherry, fed us a really good stew, bread with real butter, and strong coffee with thick cream. LeForge was by then running a farm and had cows, so he made a pretty good thing of selling milk, cream, and butter in a country where none of those items were seen very often, especially fresh. I learned that LeForge had been a farm kid before he ran away from home and came West. I was to learn a lot about him because that night led to my becoming a member of his family for a while. It came about, as I said, because I shared LeForge's love of fishing. That subject came up after we ate and smoked some more.

LeForge said: "How would you two like to go fishing with me tomorrow? They're running."

I didn't know what running was and didn't care; I simply liked to fish. It turned out he was talking about trout, with which I was then unfamiliar.

"Not me," Smith said. "Fishin' ain't my thing. Hunting, maybe."

"We can do that, too, if you stay over a while. Lots of elk and deer and even a grizzly or two around, now and then. Bears don't last long. They make good grease and prime sleeping robes, if you know how to tan one. Cherry, here, does."

That's how I ended up coming around to his cabin first thing the next morning, and how I made a move that changed my whole life for the next year and a little more.

LeForge fixed me up with a fishpole and some bait. In those days fish would bite on anything so we didn't need fancy flies, though I got to be a fly-fishing nut over the years. I'd still like to have had a fling at it in a mountain stream like the Yellowstone and some of its tributaries in those old days. I went at it in earnest, pulled out a couple of dozen without saying anything. He must have liked that. I've seen fishermen who can't throw in a line without bazooing at whoever is with them and I always thought it scared away the fish.

LeForge pulled out about the same number of trout I did, and finally, figuring we had enough, said: "Let's take these up and let Cherry clean them and fix us a mess for breakfast."

"Suits me," I told him. "I could eat a horse by now."

What a breakfast it was! I can remember it yet and almost taste it. Fresh fried trout, fried spuds, eggs fresh from his flock, thick slices of bread with butter, and some kind of homemade wild berry jam, and, of course, coffee. No meal was complete on the frontier without coffee. Some would almost as soon have done without tobacco as coffee. I never went that far.

After breakfast we went outside on his front porch and settled into some chairs he'd built himself that would outdo the best camp chairs you can buy today. We took a cup of coffee with us and smoked our pipes while we sucked in the rare mountain air and enjoyed some of the finest scenery anywhere on earth. That's my idea of what heaven ought to be like.

"I seen yore hoss, Tom," he said. "You must be pretty good with hosses."

"Fair," I said, not wanting to brag, but by then I could handle most of them.

After being quiet a while he asked: "How would you like a job? I need a good man to help me break some hosses, and just work around here. Injuns don't take to farm work, although the damned government thinks it's gonna make farmers out of them and civilize 'em." He snorted. "Civilize, my ass! They're already more civilized than the average white will ever be. They oughta leave 'em alone, feed 'em when game runs out . . . which it will in a few years . . . and let them turn to farming when they damned well don't have any choice. They'll take to it if it boils down to that to get some spending money. Besides, they're good with stock. They make a damned sight better cattlemen than farmers."

"How come you don't get one to train your horses?"

"I sell 'em mostly to people that speak English," he said.

That made sense. But I still wasn't sure I could do it and mentioned why. "I ain't so sure how Mike'll take to me deserting him. He's been pretty good to me."

"I done talked it over with him already. One of the reasons I need a man right now is I'm losin' one that used to work for Mike. He can go out with him in your place."

That's how I got to live in Paradise for a while. I don't normally look back and wish I could live this or that over, but I'd go back up there and work for LeForge in a minute if I was young again. It was a real education in surviving comfortably outdoors in that rugged territory. I learned to hunt and live off the country. Besides, I learned the Crow lingo and how to blend into the land like they could. It came in handy sooner than I expected.

I gentled horses for LeForge, who was one of the best hands with them that I ever knew. Talking to a horse, he could walk up slow and put his hand on it. I saw him do it to some wild-eyed ones that spooked at everyone that came near them. Some people have that gift, and there are few of them. After he got a green horse so it would stand for him, he'd say something in its ear that no one else could hear, and the horse would start listening—you could tell it was. I was a fair hand with horses myself and tried to pick that up from him, but I think you have to be born with it. He was the only person I ever saw get right on Buns and make him walk out without so much as trying to crow hop.

The first time he rode Buns, he brought him back and took out the spade bit. "You don't need this," he said.

"You mean *you* don't need it," I told him.

"Nobody will need it if you train the horse right."

That's where Buns and I started school together. With LeForge in the corral with us, he didn't offer to put a foot wrong and never tried to bite me once. In a month I had a new horse. I could ride him bareback without a bridle or so much as a headstall of any kind. I could control him with my legs and by a few words, such as "walk", "trot", "lope", "run", "easy" to slow him up, and "whoa" to stop him.

LeForge fixed up an Indian bridle for us, which was only a piggin' string in his mouth. "To use when you want to be quiet as a mouse," LeForge explained. He taught me how to give gentle jerks on it that amounted to the voice commands. "Besides that, it won't get caught up in the brush like reins will. Important if you're hauling yer freight in a helluva hurry, especially in the dark."

LeForge also taught me how to get Buns to come with a special whistle that he soon learned was for him only. "You can use the whistle if some Injun steals your hoss," LeForge told me. "It's OK to follow a thief and sneak up at night, but then you have to go into the herd and find your own hoss. Better to get close and whistle for him. He might get half a dozen others to follow him, and the chances of yer gettin' caught are slim. By daylight you can be forty miles away."

It all sounded good to me.

In addition to gentling horses, I farmed right alongside of LeForge, got out firewood for the winter, mended whatever needed mending, and made a lot of Crow acquaintances—a good number of them became real friends such as Mitch Boyer, who wasn't exactly a Crow but half Sioux, and whose father had been a French trapper. Of course, old-timers like Mitch would have been leery of a greenhorn like me, but working for LeForge and having his approval helped. LeForge was sort of a big stick and acted as go-between for them with the Indian agent, Clapp.

Another absolutely necessary thing to survive in the West was hunting. LeForge took me out at least once a week, and we never came back empty-handed. He always worked into the wind, if he moved at all, and would sneak up to the top of ridges and peek over from behind some cover. But best of all was learning where the game came and how to sit still and let it come to you. He was impressed with my shooting, thanks to what Captain French had taught me, especially my pistol shooting. Very few in the West had the time and money to practice with a pistol and get good at hitting something with it. LeForge was an exception, but he wasn't any better than I was at that.

That's the way things went on through the late summer

and fall, and then the winter of 1875. I was having the time of my life and hoped it would go on forever. But the snake always manages to find a way into any Garden of Eden.

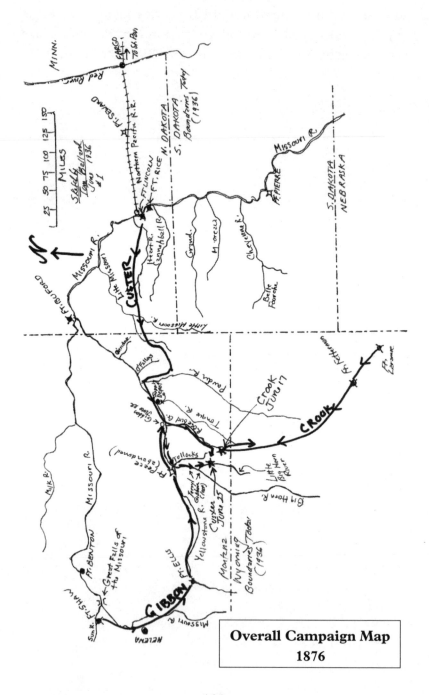

**Overall Campaign Map
1876**

Chapter Twelve

It was no secret in the West, even among the wild Plains Tribes, that Washington D.C., meaning Grant, the Great White Father, had decided his Indian policy was a bust and that the final solution would be to turn loose the Army and force the roaming tribes onto reservations. The evidence was plain from what had been done on the Southern Plains in 1874. News traveled between tribes, even if they weren't friendly, by means of the "moccasin telegraph".

When the Crows got wind of a campaign to break the power of the Sioux, they liked the idea since the Sioux were their traditional enemies and they had nothing to fear from the Army. They were already peacefully settled on a reservation and were fairly well adjusted to it. They'd been one of the few tribes that had never had any *real* trouble with whites. They may not have loved them, but they never fought them as the Blackfeet and Sioux and Cheyennes had, all traditional enemies of the Crows, who had raided them and fought them for years. So the Crows were anxious to see these tribes, especially the Sioux, headed for their come-uppance. The Sioux still made it difficult for the Crows to hunt buffalo when I first came to live with LeForge, since both tribes depended on a common hunting ground east of Crow country in the area around the mouths of the Tongue and Rosebud and Bighorn, where those rivers ran into the Yellowstone from the south.

I'd been happily living for eight months with LeForge and

Cherry and even had a room of my own in their cabin when Washington stuck its nose into our affairs in a big way. LeForge's was the first real home that I'd had since Pa had taken us West and disappeared in St. Paul and I didn't want to leave it, so, when it looked like a big Indian campaign might change that, I didn't welcome the idea.

We heard along about the end of March that General Gibbon was due to campaign against the Sioux and was coming to the reservation in hopes of recruiting Crow scouts to go with his command. It didn't sound like anything I'd be crazy about doing. The Army's by-the-book way of doing things rubbed me wrong.

But my happy days with LeForge were about to come to an end when Mitch Boyer came over one morning and LeForge invited him in for coffee and a smoke. After a while he told us what was on his mind: "General Gibbon asked me to come down to his camp. He wants a bunch of Crow scouts to go with him on a campaign after the Sioux."

LeForge asked: "What do you aim to do?"

"What do you think about it?"

Before answering, LeForge studied the ceiling, appearing to be deep in thought. Finally he said: "He'll get a bunch of young braves, no matter what we say. He'll offer them a deal they can't turn down. We might just as well go along with him, but we could drag our feet and get the best deal for the Crows that we can. I've got a score or two against the Sioux myself. I may go along, if he offers me a job."

Boyer laughed. "Oh, he'll offer *you* a job all right. Are you sure you want to go on a summer campaign and leave Cherry here to take care of the place by herself?"

"Tom-Two, here'll, help out. He knows enough to run the whole shebang by now." He looked over at me to see how that sat.

"Suits me," I said. "I never lost anything with the Army."

Boyer said: "From what I hear we'll be joining up with Custer later on. You sure you won't want to go along and see the Custers again?"

He mentioned that because I'd told him how I got to know the Custers and that Tom Custer had given me Buns. I hadn't known that Autie Custer would be coming up our way, and it did throw a different light on the idea of my joining the campaign. I'd have liked a chance to thank the Custer boys for Buns, if nothing else. But it didn't take a whole summer to do that. I could just as well go down in the fall on a boat from Fort Benton and spend a few days with them at Fort Lincoln. That way I could thank Libbie, too. So I said: "I don't want to leave Tom and Cherry in the lurch, and I can see the Custers on a visit after the work's done here next fall."

Boyer said: "If we run into as many Sioux as we're apt to, a lot of us might not see next fall."

What a prophet he turned out to be. I wonder if he had a premonition of his own fate. Indians are funny that way. And, come to think of it, I wonder if he had a premonition of what was going to happen to the Custer boys. If he did, he was more of a fatalist than I am. I'd have bought a ticket to New York City if I thought being near the Sioux would get me killed. But then, as I said, I wasn't cut out for the Army.

That was in early April, as I recall. Boyer went down to Gibbon's camp and came back the next day with the general and some other officers, escorted by Lieutenant Bradley. I wasn't sure I wanted to meet either Gibbon or Bradley again. They might be sore that I'd cut out on them. I still didn't trust the Army not to put me in chains and send me back to Terry as though I were his runaway ward. Cotillion still wasn't my idea of how I'd like to spend the rest of my days. So I avoided them both until the next day when I couldn't resist the temptation of watching Gibbon dicker with the Crow head chiefs. By then LeForge had prompted them how to deal with a starchy dude like the general and how to get the top buck in pay out of him.

I really did want to hear how Gibbon dealt with the Indians, because by then I'd come to know their ways pretty well. When I decided to write this recollection, I had a typescript made for me of Lieutenant Bradley's records of the meeting, the original of which had been in the Montana Historical Society since 1881.

Present were many chiefs and sub-chiefs, and I knew them all slightly, some better than others. The most important one was named Blackfoot. But the names are all so rare and colorful and typical of Indian names that I want to record them for my readers, in case this ever gets published. They were Tin Belly, Iron Bull, Bull-That-Goes-Hunting, Show-His-Face, Medicine Wolf, Old Onion, Mountain Pocket, Crane-In-The-Sky, Sees-All-Over-The-Land, One Feather, Spotted Horse, Long Snake, Frog, Small Beard, Curly, Shot-In-The-Jaw, White Forehead, Old Crow, Old Dog, White Mouth, and Crazy Head.

Gibbon and his staff sat at the front of the long room, and spectators sat on benches, including what Bradley called "riff-raff", myself undoubtedly among that number. I got a pretty sharp look from both him and Gibbon, after Bradley spotted me in the crowd and pointed me out to the general. I expected to hear from them before the assembly broke up.

This is how Bradley's diary reported what went on next: **The chiefs having come forward and shaken hands all around, Mr. Clapp said: "General Gibbon, commanding the Military District and expedition against** the Sioux, is here to talk with the chiefs and principal soldiers."

General Gibbon: "I have come down here to make war on the Sioux. The Sioux are your enemy and ours. For a long while they have been killing white men and killing Crows. I am going to punish the Sioux for making war upon the white man. If the Crows want to make war upon the Sioux, now is their time. If they want to drive them from their country and prevent them from sending war parties into their country to murder their men, now is their time. If they want to get revenge for the Crows that have fallen, to get revenge for the killing of such men as the gallant soldier, Long Horse, now is their time.

"White men and red men make war in a different way. The white man goes through the country with his head down and sees nothing. The red man keeps his eyes open and can see better than a white man. Now, I want some young warriors of the Crow tribe to go along with me, who will use their eyes and tell me what they see. I don't want men who will be willing to ride along with my men and stay with the wagons – I have plenty of those. I want young, active, brave men, who will be my eyes. I want twenty-five such men, men who will find out where the Sioux are so that I can go after them. They will be soldiers of the Government, get soldier's pay and soldier's food, and, when I come back, will come back with me and join their tribe again."

When he finished, LeForge who was seated next to me whispered in my ear: "I wonder who the hell wrote that bullshit for him? It sounds like Fenimore Cooper." I was surprised he'd ever read Cooper, but recalled that the Leatherstocking series was already out when he was a boy in school.

Bradley's diary went on: **The general resumed his seat, and for some time the chiefs sat silent with bowed heads. At length the general informed them that he was ready to hear what they had to say.**

This shows how much he knew about Indians. It might have taken a week to get an answer, and, if he pushed, he might never get one. The chiefs were being polite that day, and Old Crow reproached him very mildly: "You have said what you had to say . . . don't be too fast! We are studying within ourselves and will talk after a while."

Then White Mouth got something off his chest that had bothered all the Crows, and it was as good a comment as you'll find about what the Crows thought of the white man's way of making war against the Sioux. And let's not forget they had seen the Army run off the Bozeman Trail and made to close three forts all within the decade because of the harassment of the Sioux under Red Cloud. These Crows had a hearty respect for the Sioux as fighting men, and almost no respect for the Army.

White Mouth said: "The old man [Gibbon] is only talking. You have already been down below, our young men went with you, and you turned back after a while without doing anything. We are afraid that you will do it again."

Gibbon explained that the raid they referred to—a rescue mission after the men at Fort Pease—hadn't intended to go farther and had accomplished its mission. He said that, if they had encountered the Sioux, they would have fought them.

Blackfoot made quite a long speech and said he was in favor of the young Crows going with Gibbon, but that they wouldn't listen to him if he told them to do it, that the decision was theirs, and he would be in favor of it if the decision was yes, and accept it if it was no, but that, should they go, they will want white men with them "who can speak the language. It will be well to have such men along. . . ."

He had quite a bit more to say, but most of it was about short rations, a perennial complaint of all the Indian tribes—and justified, I might add, from my own observation.

It was my first experience watching how the Army got interpretation of English to an Indian tribe. I could have done as well, or better, myself. The problem was that the interpreters could handle the Indian tongue pretty well, but were deficient in English.

As I expected, Bradley cornered me before I could escape, grabbing my arm and smiling. "We heard you were down here. General Terry sends his best regards."

That sank in for what it really meant, which was that Gibbon was still looking after me.

"We missed you," he continued, "but General Gibbon said to tell you he, for one, understands. He was pretty wild himself at your age."

I thought—*I'll bet!*—but I was actually glad to see Brad, since I liked him a lot.

He went on and asked a question I should have lied about. "Have you learned much Crow lingo while you've been down here."

"I get by," I said.

"Good. How would you like come along with us as an interpreter. We'll pay you more than an interpreter gets by putting you on the books, at a hundred a month, as a forage master?"

I'd have liked a hundred a month if I had to peel potatoes. That was real money in those days. And I knew what a forage master was. He was someone with the political connections to suck at a public teat. Bos Custer was a good example.

"I'll have to check with Tom LeForge," I told Brad. "He's counting on me to look after his place if he goes with you."

"He hasn't been asked."

I realized then I might have cost LeForge a job that he would have liked. He and Mitch Boyer were pretty close and I suspected he wanted to go along with Boyer for the adventure as well as a little extra cash. Young as I was, I'd learned a few things about haggling by then and saw a way to keep Brad happy and at the same time avoid cheating LeForge out of a job he probably wanted.

"I'll go," I said, "on two conditions."

Brad's face got that military look that all officers have when it appears their wishes are going to be opposed. "Shoot," he said.

"I'll take the job if you hire LeForge, too, if he wants to go along. He speaks Crow like one of them. I don't, but I get by. And, come to think of it, in case you're going to pay me more than him, don't let him know it."

"I'll run it by the general," he said.

But I knew what the answer would be. I was sure, even then, that Terry had told them to get me back under the Army's wing, and already had plans to get me safely back to St. Paul when the campaign was over, if not sooner.

Later that day LeForge came home and found me working in the barn, cleaning harness and oiling it. He sat down on a stump we used as a bench and filled his pipe carefully, got it lit, and then opened up. I could tell he had something on his mind and was waiting.

"I met General Gibbon," he said for an ante.

"Oh? How did he strike you?"

"Like an Army general."

"And how is that?"

"A starchy asshole."

I laughed. I couldn't have put it better myself. Custer was the only one I ever met who didn't completely fit the mold.

There had to be more than that and I waited for it.

Finally LeForge said in a sort of wondering voice: "I got a pretty funny proposition from him. He said he'd like to hire me as an interpreter, provided I let you come along as a forage master."

I almost laughed out loud, but managed to hold it in. "What did you tell him?"

"I said it was OK with me if it was with you. What do you say?"

I thought of the hundred a month and balanced it against the chances of my getting the hell kicked out of me by the troops who surely remembered me as "teacher's pet", and figured I could keep clear of them day or night, especially with what I'd been learning about being sneaky from the Indians. In fact, that thought sweetened the kitty on taking the job; it suggested to me that I ought to get even, one at a time, on dark nights. I knew who every one of the bastards had been. I thought: *I'll give you sonsabitches a waltz before the campaign is over.* I did, too, but that's not relevant to my story.

According to Bradley's diary, I joined the campaign on April 13th, not a Friday, by the way, although it should have been. Brad had mentioned that "LeForgey", as he insisted on spelling Tom's name, hadn't got there but was due with one additional Crow. Someone must have told him LeForge was bringing a Crow, not realizing it was me.

To borrow another really useful expression from my current G.I. friends, the Montana Column, as it was called, mostly "fucked off" for a couple of months. Buns and I had a picnic most of the time, riding with Brad's Crow scouts. The scouts thought Brad was pretty funny and so did I. Here's an example of why: One night a sentry fired at a log in the river, mistaking it for a Sioux swimming across the Yellowstone to steal a horse or two. Naturally all of his Crow scouts rolled out, as well as the mounted infantry assigned to him. Brad had them slither up to the riverbank in the dark, and then he came with a lantern and peered into the bulrushes to see if he could spot an interloper for them to shoot. His diary doesn't tell it that way, but that's the way it really happened. He could be really green sometimes, but we all liked him.

LeForge thought it was the dumbest thing he'd ever seen in his life, but he didn't say so. Brad was likable for a lot of things, such as seeing that his scouts got plenty to eat and weren't mistreated by the soldiers.

Our orders were to keep the Sioux south of the Yellowstone until the other two forces of the pincers were able to come up and trap them. Gibbon had orders from Terry not to bring on a big fight until the reinforcements got there, if he could avoid it, but only Gibbon knew that and it was to cause a lot of dissatisfaction, at least among my Crow friends, when it seemed we were avoiding a fight. If I'd been a soldier, I'd have welcomed staying as far away from the hostiles as I could. In view of what happened later in the campaign, I don't think anyone needs a lecture to justify my attitude. Custer's 7th was to lose half its strength in one day, 262 killed outright, 6 dying later, and 66 wounded.

When LeForge heard that we were going to "contain" the Sioux, he laughed out loud. "Jesus Christ," he snorted, "the whole damn' kit and caboodle of them could cross over the river twenty miles from us any night, and we wouldn't find it out till the next day, if then. If they crossed on our back trail, we might not find it out for a week, until somebody came up with the mail or something."

He liked Bradley all right but thought he was a real goose when it came to scouting, although he always gave him credit for guts. I'll vouch for the fact that he was a man of great courage, to the point of foolhardiness, and it finally got him killed the next year just as the same trait brought Custer down.

A lot happened while we stumbled around "keeping the Indians south of the Yellowstone", but not much of real importance. We were marking time. I'm going to cover just a couple more incidents, then get to the events immediately leading up to Custer's Last Stand. These two incidents are worth remembering since they give a good example of how the "Indian fighting" Army fumbled while out on a campaign in the first case, and in the second how I killed my first man, a Sioux warrior.

Chapter Thirteen

After a month or so, the troops and horses were getting hardened up, but the Army still didn't know beans about Indian fighting. They needed to practice their trade every day, but, when the troops were in quarters, especially in the winter, they mostly practiced chopping wood, building additions to the forts, playing poker, dominoes, checkers, euchre, and cribbage, and drinking if liquor could be had. A few were even readers. By spring the men were soft as butter and so were their cavalry horses. The work horses were hard because they were used almost every day, and it goes without saying that the cavalry horses should have been, as well as the troops.

Some of the new men hadn't even shot their guns yet, and the old-timers needed to practice regularly. Shooting is like bowling or tennis—you've got to practice constantly if you want to get and stay good at it, especially with a pistol as Captain French had shown me. Congress never appropriated enough money for practice ammunition and hardly enough to fight with, and, in addition, a lot of Army officers, from the top down, thought target practice was a waste of time. Along those lines, General Sherman, the Army's top dog, was rumored to have opposed repeating firearms during the Civil War because he feared the men would waste ammunition. I can't see how it could have escaped him that the repeating Spencer had won a lot of battles for the Union.

The Indians were in little better shape than our troops in

the winter, but due only to circumstances, the main one being that their horses were always puny just before grass came up. Their tough little ponies knew how to dig down through the snow for grass, but it was slow work and they never got enough to eat in the winter, which was why there were few Indian raids in cold weather. The Indians were lucky to keep the animals alive, and the poor, scrawny things learned how to strip cottonwood bark to supplement their lean diet, or any other kind of bark if they were really hungry. The Indians themselves were often low on rations by spring.

Even at that the Indians were fearsome opponents for a collection of farm boys or guttersnipes right off the city streets, especially as untrained as they always were. There was a pretty good leavening of Civil War veterans, however, and it's a good thing there was. In any case, winter was the time to hit the Indians, but it took the Army a long time to realize that and learn how to do it passably.

Because everyone knew of Indian fighting tactics and their merciless treatment of white prisoners, there was a general sense of fear in the rank and file of the whole command, and I could feel it. The officers may have thought we could whip all the Sioux on the face of the earth, but word certainly got around that our scouts, both white and red, didn't share that bravado. They'd fought the Sioux. If you were captured, you could be burned at the stake by Stone Age men who fought with absolutely no tradition of mercy. If they merely killed and scalped you, you were one of the lucky ones.

LeForge told me over and over: "Save one last bullet for yourself, if you get in a tight. Shooting yourself beats hell out of what the Sioux will do to you."

It was with that cautioning in the front of my mind that I rode with him and Brad day after day on scouting trips far from our camps, where we might have been ambushed by ten times our numbers.

Gibbon pitched our main camp at the site of abandoned Fort Pease, formerly a trading post, just below the mouth of the Big Horn. Most of the troops camped there while Gibbon sent out scouting troops of cavalry to supplement Brad's scouting. Sioux raiding parties were around us all the time and were laughing at us. They tried to steal horses almost every night, and finally they ran off the Crow scouts' horses.

I was stunned to see the Crows, grown men, standing in a doleful row, after they discovered their loss, and actually crying like babies. I figured that Indians were funnier critters than I'd thought and that I still had a lot to learn about them. I couldn't imagine a hardened white scout acting like that. I had a hard time not laughing and said in a low voice to LeForge: "Actually they're pretty funny."

"There's nothing funny about losing your horse out here."

"I mean crying over it like a kid."

"Buns was with their ponies," LeForge said, pokerfaced.

I figured he was pulling my leg. "The hell he was, I put him with the cavalry herd."

"Ask them," LeForge said, pointing at the Crow scouts. "I saw Buns out there just before dark and thought you were getting to be as foolish as a real Crow."

I didn't doubt him and began to feel like a *real* Crow—I wanted to go over and cry with the rest of them. I guess it hadn't occurred to me that any of the Crows would love a particular horse as I did Buns. I scouted around, anyhow, in a hopeless attempt to find him and came back empty-handed. I was seeing red and wanted to go after the sonsabitches that stole him. LeForge must have read my mind. He took me along when he looked up Brad, telling him: "How about gettin' the kid a horse, and borrowing a couple more for some of them Crows, and we'll try to get their hosses back. They ain't gonna be worth a damn to you on foot."

Brad loaned me his second best horse, a big Thoroughbred named Raven, who belied his color; he was a gray, and damned fast.

"I'll give you about ten minutes start," Brad said, "then I'll take the boys, and any Crows I can beg horses for, and come across the river to get the Sioux's attention."

By the "boys" he meant our white scout detachment of about twenty men, volunteers borrowed from the various cavalry companies. The odds were that the Sioux horse thieves would leave a scout or two behind to watch their back trail.

So LeForge, I, and three Crows followed the stolen horses' tracks, keeping out of sight as much as possible in the trees along the river. The trail led east on the north bank for a few miles, and then we found where they'd taken to the water. I was surprised that Buns hadn't rebelled about then and turned back, but he was used to being with the Crow horses, and probably went along due to herd instinct. We continued downstream for a couple of miles, beyond where the horse thieves had crossed and swam over.

A word here about those Western novels that tell how cowboys rode their swimming horses across the Cimarron, or some other river. If you're on your horse when he hits swimming water, he's going to go under and take you with him. You might get kicked in the head underwater and it'll be your last swim.

I'd already been across swimming water before with LeForge on hunting trips. He'd told me: "You get your damned boots off, and anything else that can pull you under, tie them behind your saddle, and get off before you hit real deep water. Be sure you swim on the upstream side of the nag and hold onto a stirrup. Tie the reins to the pommel of your saddle, too, so neither you nor the horse get tangled up in them, and so you can grab them as soon as the horse hits bottom again . . . otherwise, he might decide to cut out as soon as he feels land."

After crossing the water, LeForge and I put our boots back on while the Crows watched disgustedly, then we all cautiously mounted the bluff on the south side and almost ran directly into our horse thieves. We pulled back just in time. They weren't looking our way since they assumed that, as usual, if anyone followed them, they'd take a long time getting organized to do it and certainly wouldn't be quick enough to be in front of them. The reason we were always so slow was that we had to get Gibbon's approval to cross more than one or two men at a time.

This time LeForge had said to Brad: "The hell with getting God's blessing first, we're going to get the kid's horse back!" It was the kind of music Brad liked, and he'd been itching for a reason to ignore Gibbon. "God" was the irreverent name the troops applied to Gibbon, a nickname first conferred by Doctor Paulding, the regiment's surgeon. And not because of Gibbon's bearded, Old Testament appearance, either. Paulding had a sharp tongue, and Gibbon acted like he thought he was omnipotent.

Anyhow, the Sioux thieves hadn't expected anyone to head them off, so they weren't even moving very fast. I spotted Buns before we scrambled out of sight and instantly saw red. All I thought of was getting him back even if I had to fight the whole bunch of them single-handed. A real brilliant (stupid) idea grabbed me, and I gave my special whistle to call Buns.

LeForge growled: "You dumb son-of-a-bitch, are you trying to get us killed?"

I paid no attention to him and rode back up the incline to see if Buns was coming. What I saw chilled me. He was coming all right, but not flat out, just loping along, not realizing that a Sioux was closing behind him, trying to turn him back. The Indian may not even have heard my whistle. But when he saw he wasn't gaining on Buns fast enough to overtake him before he would be over the crest of the bluff, he whipped up his buffalo bow, and I had no doubt what he had in mind—*If I can't have him, neither can anyone else.*

I'd heard the Indians could shoot an arrow completely through a tough buffalo bull with one of those short bows. So I jerked out my Henry and hoped I'd be quick enough. While I was watching, the Sioux had already whipped an arrow after Buns and was notching another, his first shot, from a little too far away, had fallen short. Luckily for me and Buns, he decided to try getting a little closer for the second shot.

I wasn't sure I could drop the Sioux at that range, so, although I hate to shoot horses, I shot his horse out from under him. The Sioux lit hard, jumped up, startled by my shot, and looked around. When he spotted me, he must have figured I'd never be there unless I was backed up by a large number of others, so he took off as fast as he could. I jumped off Raven for a steadier shot, snapped a round after him, and it was probably the luckiest shot I ever made. The range had to be two hundred yards and the Henry wasn't really accurate much above a hundred. But even at that range the heavy .44 slug drove the runner onto his face, and he never quivered once.

When I was sure Buns would follow me, I jumped back on Raven. My heart jumped into my mouth at the sight of about a dozen Sioux coming my way, urging their ponies to a flat-out run. I headed for the crest of the bluff and found only LeForge waiting. As I rode up, he yelled: "Let's get the hell out of here! You stirred up a hornet's nest." I didn't look back to see. He let off a parting shot from his buffalo rifle to discourage pursuit. The Sioux had a hearty respect for the gun that shot a mile and carried a bullet as big as the end of a man's finger and they knew its sound—no one could mistake that big boom for any other rifle.

"Dropped a horse," LeForge grunted as we scrambled down the shale slope, slipping all the way with our horses squatted on their rumps. We reached the water's edge in time to see our Crows in midstream, heading for safety. Our horses took to the water in one jump, Buns right beside us. It was only then that I started to be really scared and could feel my heart pounding my ribs like a trip hammer.

Swimming a river is slow business and seems a lot slower when you're expecting a shower of lead to rain down on you any second. I swam as low in the water as I could and wondered what a bullet felt like when it tore into you. That's when Buns, in true form, decided to complicate things. He was coming right along behind me, got a hoof in my pant cuff, and pulled me under. I still held like a vice to Raven's stirrup, and, when I surfaced, I yelled back at Buns: "Get the hell back a ways, goddammit!"

He seemed to understand and gave me a little more space. I was still waiting for a slug to tear into me and was breathing raggedly. It didn't make for good swimming. Then I wasted some more breath and said: "I'm supposed to ride you, you son-of-a-bitch, you ain't supposed to try to ride me."

This pickle was one of the trickiest things I'd ever got caught in and it convinced me that campaigning with the Army wasn't all it was cracked up to be in dime novels.

We made it across before the Sioux got brave enough to come over the crest, probably due to LeForge having cut down that horse—they "heap savvied" buffalo rifles. When they finally got up their nerve, they began popping up like ducks in a shooting gallery from behind the crest, one at a time, till there were a couple of dozen of them. Cold and soaked, but in one piece, LeForge and I moved away right smart in among the brush and trees.

The Sioux took a few random shots at us. When I looked back, I could make them out, shaking their fists and making obscene gestures to suggest ramming something up us where it would hurt most, but I didn't hear a single bullet clip the nearby branches or ricochet off a rock, both of which you can damned well hear when they happen.

LeForge stopped, dismounted, and got behind a tree, taking his Sharps with him. He steadied it against the tree and squeezed off a shot. After a second I saw one of those bastards topple off his horse and bite the dust. You can bet the rest pulled out of sight in a hurry.

I said: "That was one helluva shot, Tom."

He grinned. "It ain't hard with one of these babies."

The Crows, who saw the Sioux bite the dust, were grinning from ear to ear and chattering congratulations as LeForge hopped back on his horse and we cut out again. It wasn't time to let down our guard, though. You never knew when the Sioux would circle around and come after you in earnest, especially if you'd shot some popular chief or a heap big warrior.

They might well have done that, but it wasn't long before we heard more firing from over near the crest.

LeForge said: "It's probably Brad and the boys. Most likely slipped up while the Sioux were watchin' us, and jumped them from behind. The damn' fool. There might be a couple of hundred of them over there." But he didn't sound too unhappy. "I hope he's not fool enough to follow that bunch if they run."

Somehow I didn't feel like going back to reinforce them just then, or ever as far as that went. We were a mile or so from the crest before my heart slowed down. I felt pretty good about getting Buns back, but then it flashed into my mind what an unpredictable critter he was. He was just as apt to decide to go back and join the herd as not.

I yelled at LeForge: "I've got to stop a minute!"

He gave me a what-the-hell-for glance, and then a look of worry passed over his face, perhaps thinking I'd been hit.

"I want to switch over to Buns," I explained.

He slowed, surveying our back trail and the bluffs south of the river, before he agreed.

We got back to camp a couple of hours before Brad came in. He was called directly to Gibbon's tent. On his way past us, he gave us a look that said: "I guess I'm in for my lumps." I didn't envy him.

LeForge clapped me on the shoulder, having forgiven me for endangering our lives like a damned fool, and it was my turn to get praised. He said: "That was a hell of a couple of shots you made with a damned Henry popgun."

"Luck," I said.

"Maybe."

In any case, what he was thinking was plain in his eyes. On the frontier the experienced ones always had reservations about greenhorns like me until they had proved themselves, and the preferred way to do that was by killing someone "that needed it". That was my first notch, you might say, though I never carved one on any of my guns. It wouldn't be my last notch, either, and I'm not ashamed of any of them and was damned proud of that one. I felt absolutely no remorse over killing my first man. Nothing. I was simply glad I got Buns back. From then on I made sure he was close herded with the cavalry horses, and, if he'd had a chance to graze during the day, at night I tied him right next to where I slept.

My turn for an ass chewing from Gibbon came a little while later. LeForge went with me.

"Well," Gibbon said, spearing me with a frosty eye, "what have you got to say for yourself?"

I said pretty lamely: "About what?"

"About what?" he roared in his best God-like voice. "About dragging that damned fool Bradley across the river."

"I thought he went after the Crows' horses," I said.

"He went to keep you from getting killed!"

That hadn't occurred to me. I never suspected the lieutenant actually liked me that much. I knew why Gibbon didn't want me killed.

Gibbon's cold eyes came to rest on LeForge. "And *you*," he said, pointing a long, accusing finger at Tom, "you of all people should have had sense enough to keep the kid safe."

LeForge wasn't ruffled even slightly. He said: "From what I saw the kid doesn't need anyone to keep him safe."

Bradley hadn't known what I had done when he went to see Gibbon, so Gibbon was still in the dark about the fight from our side. Finally he cooled down a little and asked LeForge: "What makes you say that?"

LeForge recited our whole adventure. I thought Gibbon was trying to conceal an approving look. When LeForge was finished, Gibbon looked me over as though he'd never seen me before. "Well, I'll be go to hell!" he said. Then he added, almost to himself: "Don't that beat a hog flying?"

Looking back from years of experience with big shots like him, I think he wanted to get us out of there before he appeared almost human.

In any case, he said abruptly: "Get the hell out of here, you two damned fools! And don't pull any shenanigans like that ever again!"

LeForge and I walked away, not sadder or wiser. "Did you notice that the old son-of-a-bitch could hardly keep from grinning?" LeForge commented. "He's got his good side. Whatever you say for him, he fought a helluva war when he was in his prime."

That remark about "whatever you say for him" had to do with the fact that Gibbon had been avoiding a big fight with the Sioux. We didn't know that his orders from Terry had forbidden it, unless he figured he had a sure chance to catch them off guard and wipe out a village.

Soon after, Gibbon tried to do just that by attacking the big Sioux village that Brad finally discovered. We knew there had to be one around, what with all the Sioux pestering us. Gibbon figured it was probably over on the Tongue River to the east, and he was right. Brad risked his neck again and found it for him.

I didn't get to go on the search, because LeForge and I went back up the river with Lieutenant Roe's company to look for a Diamond R wagon train that was overdue with supplies, and escort it in.

Chapter Fourteen

I've been scribbling my story on a lined pad when the mood strikes me, usually late at night after I wake up from my after-dinner nap and before I get ready for bed. (Sleeping is important at my age.) Sometimes I sip a cognac and rummage around in my memory for what to say next. I was doing that last night and got quite a shock.

A familiar voice said: "Tom-Two, for Christ's sake cut to the chase. I've heard enough about old Granny Gibbon and his crowd."

I looked around to see where the high-pitched voice was coming from, but nothing was in sight, naturally, because the voice was Autie's, clear as could be and just the way I remembered it. I wasn't surprised. In fact, I figured I was still dreaming. Then I realized I was awake, and thought: How neat. A spook.

I collected my wits and asked: "When the hell did you take up cussing? And where are you?"

"I never gave it up. Just swore off swearing for a while. And I'm over here."

I saw the cognac bottle rise and pour out a generous slug into a snifter glass. The snifter then rose as magically as the bottle had. The level came down a ways, but I never have figured out where the cognac disappeared.

"You never drank, either."

"Never gave it up, either, just put off the next time, like

*cussing. Besides, you and those G.I.s that hang out here are a bad
example for an innocent . . . or maybe a good example, come to
think of it. It's pretty confining to be a straight arrow all the time."*

"Like Terry?"

"Yeah, like Daisy."

I couldn't help but laugh.

"What's so funny?"

*"So you've been around, eavesdropping. And I might add that
you never struck me as exactly a straight arrow. Your brother
Tom, maybe."*

"Tom? He was the original hell raiser!"

*"I noticed that once or twice, now that you mention it. I was
just trying to be funny. Did you know that he and Tom Rosser both
got drunk as lords and passed out in your teetotalling quarters at
Fort Lincoln when I went through there the last time?"*

"Where the hell was I?"

*"Hobnobbing with Lawrence Barrett and Shakespeare in New
York. Which reminds me . . . to answer your question, I've been
toe dancing around with this story, putting off the chase while I
sketch in the* dramatis personæ, *you might say."*

"Jesus! You've really been flying high since I saw you last.
Dramatis personæ, *eh? I wouldn't even know what it means if I
hadn't hung around with the likes of Barrett. So now that you've
got them sketched in, let's get with it."*

*"How would you suggest I do that? I've sort of been mulling it
over and can't decide."*

*"You take out with your tall tale right now and start up the
Rosebud like we did, and this time, as we go along, I might break
in and tell you what I was thinking from time to time."*

"Good. By the way, how is Libbie?"

"Fine as wine."

*I watched as another cognac poured itself and disappeared in
mid-air. The snifter glass floated down to the table. I must have*

dozed off again, because the next thing I remember is getting up and going to bed. I didn't go right to sleep. Old Autie's spook had given me a lot to think about—and look forward to.

1876

The Yellowstone

We got word that Terry, rather than Custer, would be coming personally to command the Dakota Column, as the troops leaving from Fort Lincoln were called. President Grant was pissed off at Custer for implicating Grant's brother in a scandal being investigated by Congress. He wanted to relieve Custer of command and cut him out of the campaign entirely.

Finally Generals Terry and Sheridan succeeded in getting Custer restored to the limited command of the 7th only, but not of the whole Dakota Column as had been intended. They had different reasons for wanting Custer. Terry had wanted to stay comfortably at home. What happened must have peeved Terry a heap, since it cut into his busy summer social season in St. Paul. Besides, the rugged country they'd be campaigning in didn't lend itself to riding around in a buggy being driven by Captain Hughes. Next best, Terry wanted Custer along so he wouldn't have to work too hard. Sheridan, on the other hand, wanted Custer along because he recognized the lazy streak in Terry. Sheridan expected someone to do some fighting.

Gibbon got orders to go down the river and meet Terry on the steamer, *Far West*—steamers beat hell out of even a buggy. Terry made sure that Gibbon brought me along.

Christ, I thought, *am I headed back for cotillion?*

My suspicions were aroused when Gibbon told me the general specified that my horse be brought along, too. He grinned when he told me, saying: "It looks like you'll be headed for West Point when this campaign is over."

I envisioned me *and* Buns in irons. I didn't mind leaving, however, because LeForge's horse had taken a spill and Tom had broken his collar bone. I liked Brad OK, but didn't trust him without LeForge riding with him and advising him, and it would be a while before LeForge got on a horse again.

Once on the *Far West,* Buns had his say about being confined in a pen again on board a boat, but finally consented not to try kicking it down after I had a few words with him. The words were: "We're both going to get the hell out of here when Terry isn't watching. Probably some dark night."

I knew he understood every word I said from the wicked gleam he got in his eyes. If it came to it, we'd jump the rail and swim for it. We'd been practicing swimming in the Yellowstone all spring. After we ran for it, I intended to camp out in the hills if need be, and hook up with Custer later.

Terry was starchy with me at our reunion. Gibbon was an interested spectator, since he was in on the whole affair of my originally running away to play hooky from cotillion.

"Well, son," Terry said, extending his hand, "we all missed you. The ladies send their warm regards."

Warm? I remembered Libbie Custer's kiss and thought: *They should take lessons from her about warm.*

Terry was one of those with the knack of quickly withdrawing all but his fingertips just when a real handshake was getting started. Nonetheless, I liked him and was glad to see him. I could never forget that he had picked me out of the gutter, almost literally, and started me on the road to self-respect.

"I've got some special work for you," Terry said, "so hang around. And next time you decide to run off, come say good bye. Promise me that. I won't force you to stay anywhere. You're getting to be a man."

I wondered if he'd really noticed, or was buttering me up. "I'll let you know if I decide to quit," I told him. "I'm on the payroll, so I guess I'll just about have to do what you want."

At that he smiled. "Yes, Tom." There was mild sarcasm in his tone. "I guess I know you pretty well by now. I'll see you later and we'll have a long talk for old time's sake. If there's anything I can do for you, say so."

I thanked God that his kind remarks hadn't been the lead into another sales pitch for West Point.

"There is something you can do for me," I said. "Let me exercise my horse."

That caught him off guard, and he had little choice but to agree. He said to Gibbon: "Tell Captain Marsh that Tom can take his horse off, then send for the other officers."

I sprang Buns as quickly as I could, in case Terry changed his mind. Captain Marsh was at the head of the gangplank when I approached with Buns. He had remembered me from my trip upriver the year before and had greeted me like an old friend when I had showed up with Gibbon. Now he gave me and Buns a friendly wave as we bounced down the gangplank. "Good luck, kid," he said. He probably knew I was going to play hooky again.

I had saddled up on board, and kicked it to Buns as soon as we were clear. After we slowed down, I said: "I told you I'd get you out of jail."

He snorted and cleared his nostrils as much as to say: " 'Deed you did. Thanks."

A couple of days later Custer came in with the 7th and had

his tent pitched near the *Far West*. I had word of his approach and rode out on Buns to meet him.

"Tom-Two!" He rode up and put out his hand. There was no doubt from his expression and tone of voice that he was genuinely glad to see me. "We all missed you. Libbie said, if I saw you, to say hello and give you her love. Tom is coming along behind. Bos and Autie Reed are with him."

Autie Reed was his nephew, Armstrong Reed, son of his older half-sister.

I filled him in on what I'd been doing, and he listened carefully.

We rode a ways before he spoke, then he started his typical probing for information. "Tell me about the Indians. Do you know where they are and how many?"

"We've been scouting them for two months. You should talk to Lieutenant Bradley, who is Colonel Gibbon's chief of scouts. He spotted a big village of them a while back, over on the Tongue River. Some of Gibbon's other officers don't have much faith in Brad, but I've been working for him all spring."

"Well, those Indians aren't over on the Tongue now, or we'd have run across them. What's your opinion of Lieutenant Bradley? You must know him pretty well to be calling him Brad."

"He's a good man. Besides, he's had two first-class scouts working for him, Tom LeForge and Mitch Boyer. They've lived up here for years. I know LeForge pretty well. I worked for him last fall, up till Colonel Gibbon hired him as a scout this spring. I know Mitch, too, but not as well."

"Bring this Lieutenant Bradley over to see me tonight if you can. I'd like to talk to him privately."

From his use of opportunities such as this, it occurred to me that Custer had hunches that often helped him get ahead of others. I knew that he'd get more out of Brad alone than with Gibbon around and certainly more than with Terry listening. But, like all Army officers, Brad knew where his bread was buttered. If Gibbon found out he was seeing Custer on the sly, he'd raise hell.

I said: "I don't think Brad would want to risk coming over here to talk to you alone."

Custer asked: "Why not?"

"Because God"—the name slipped out and I couldn't take it back, so plowed on—"wouldn't want him to."

"God?"

"General Gibbon . . . it's what his men call him."

I waited for a reaction. Custer chuckled. "God, eh?" Then: "Well, see if you can talk the lieutenant into sneaking over to talk to me."

Brad was camped with the rest of Gibbon's command across the river. Terry had ordered the command back to Fort Pease, but I figured I'd be able to find Brad even if he was on the road, or at least I'd give it a try. I'd rather have brought LeForge, but he was down at Pease with his broken collar bone. Then I thought of Boyer and decided I'd bring him, if I couldn't get Brad. I didn't know yet he was going to be assigned to Custer anyhow, along with some of the Crows.

It was less trouble than I'd imagined. Brad, like most young officers, was impressed with Custer's reputation for fighting. He'd been champing at the bit to attack the Sioux all spring and wanted to see a real fighter like Custer in the flesh.

That afternoon General Terry had had a big strategy meeting on the *Far West* with Custer, Gibbon, and Gibbon's cavalry commander, Major James Brisbin. It broke up about 6:00p.m. The result of that meeting was an "order" issued to Custer that has become of major significance to the *post-*

humous destruction of his reputation. For this reason, I will reprint it here verbatim, as it was issued. I say "as it was issued" because it was later changed in respect to two significant words in Terry's order book, as I indicate:

Camp at the mouth of the Rosebud River
Montana Territory,
June 22, 1876
Lieutenant-Colonel Custer, 7th Cavalry
Colonel:
The Brigadier General Commanding directs that, as soon as your regiment can be made ready for the march, you will proceed up the Rosebud in pursuit of the Indians whose trail was discovered by Major Reno a few days since. It is, of course, impossible to give you precise instructions in regard to this movement, and were it not impossible to do so the Department Commander places too much confidence in your zeal, energy, and ability to wish to impose on you precise orders which might hamper your action when nearly in contact with the enemy. He will, however, indicate to you his own views of what your action should be, and he desires that you should conform to them unless you shall see sufficient reason [later "sufficient reason" was altered in Terry's Order Book, to "absolute necessity", probably by Captain Hughes] **for departing from them. He thinks that you should proceed up the Rosebud until you ascertain definitely the direction the trail spoken of leads. Should it be found (as it appears almost certain that it will be found) to turn to the Little Big Horn, he thinks that you should still proceed southward, perhaps as far as the headwaters of the Tongue, and then turn toward the Little Big Horn, feeling constantly, how-**

ever, to your left, so as to preclude the possibility of the escape of the Indians to the south or southeast by passing around your left flank. The column of Colonel Gibbon is now in motion for the mouth of the Big Horn. As soon as it reaches that point it will cross the Yellowstone and move up at least as far as the forks of the Big and Little Horns. Of course its future movements must be controlled by circumstances as they arise, but it is hoped that the Indians, if upon the Little Horn, will be so nearly enclosed by the two columns that their escape will be impossible. The Department Commander desires that on your way up the Rosebud you should thoroughly examine the upper part of Tullock's Creek, and that you should endeavor to send a scout through to Colonel Gibbon's column with information of the result of your examination. The lower part of the creek will be examined by a detachment of Colonel Gibbon's command. The supply steamer will be pushed up the Big Horn as far as the fork of the river if the river is found to be navigable for that distance, and the Department Commander, who will accompany the column of Colonel Gibbon, desires you to report to him there not later than the expiration of the time for which your troops are rationed, unless, in the meantime you receive further orders.

> Very respectfully your obedient servant,
> E. W. Smith
> Captain 18th Infantry
> Acting Assistant Adjutant General

Custer's cognac commentary:

"I could have ridden to Washington D.C. to see the Centennial Celebration on those orders, and any officer in the Army would

*have agreed until Terry decided to use that ambiguous masterpiece
to 'protect his ass', and crucify me."*

I knew Custer picked up that "protect his ass" business
from my WWII G.I.s. The term commonly used was PYA, for
"protect your ass", and the files commonly kept to support
your position were called "Pearl Harbor Files" after the big
investigation that followed that affair where they were
looking for and found some candidates to blame for it.

Back to the story. Although Gibbon's troops had already
started down the river, I was anxious to see how Brad and
Custer would work out together, so I swam over to find Brad.
I found him, and we came back well after dark, sort of bor-
rowing a skiff to cross the river. Brad told me that Mitch
Boyer had already been sent to Custer to act as a scout.

Prior to our arrival, Custer had had an officers' call at
which he'd issued his own orders to his company commanders to get ready to carry out Terry's desires. Some of the
officers who'd been at that officers' call reported in later writ-
ings that Custer had been edgy and crabby, but, when I got
there with Brad, he was in a good mood.

Once we were inside, Custer had the guard pull shut the
flaps of his tent and told him not to let in a soul. After a brief
hand shaking, he sat us down. Boyer was still there, having already got a preliminary grilling by Custer.

Custer said: "Boyer tells me you've had a close watch on
the Sioux all spring, which is why I wanted to talk to you."

Brad nodded. "That's true, General."

"Where do you think they are now?"

Brad looked at Boyer for some clue as to what he may have
said and got none. "Probably in the Little Big Horn country.
We've seen smoke over there the past few days. There was a

big camp of them on the Tongue, but they've moved west."

"How many?"

Brad nodded to Boyer for an answer, and the guide said: "Lots more'n I ever saw together before. Maybe four hundred lodges, but could be more."

"How many braves?"

"At least fifteen hundred, maybe more," Boyer told him. "They come out from the reservations in summer to hunt buffalo, but they usually don't camp all together the way they are now."

"Why do you think they have this big camp?"

"Probably to have a sun dance."

"Where do you think they are now?"

"I heard your Major Reno followed a trail that went over into the Little Big Horn."

"You think they're still there?"

"Nowhere else to go beyond there . . . no reason to go anywhere else. That's where the buffalo are this time of year."

"How about across the Yellowstone?"

"No. If they leave, they'll go south to the Big Horns and cut back east."

"Do they know we're here?"

Boyer laughed out loud. "Hell, General, I'd bet they been watchin' you from the minute you left Fort Lincoln. They probably have somebody back at Fort Lincoln who knows when your wife plays the piano and gets the news out here by the next morning. They call it the moccasin telegraph."

Custer shrugged. "Maybe. I believe in the moccasin telegraph. I've seen it work too often not to."

"They watched us all spring . . . played games with us, if the truth be known."

"Why didn't Gibbon attack them?"

"We heard General Terry didn't want him to," Bradley put in.

Custer looked disgusted. He was probably also surprised. If Terry had given Gibbon such orders, it was obvious he hadn't told Custer.

Custer's cognac commentary:
"Terry never let his left hand know what his right was doing. It was news to me."

Boyer added: "It's a good thing Gibbon stayed on his side of the river."

"How's that?" Custer asked.

"He'd have been wiped out," Boyer responded. "He tried to cross the river once, drowned a bunch of horses, and gave it up."

"Lieutenant Bradley, do you know what Gibbon's orders were for certain?" Custer said.

"No, sir, but I told you what we all heard. We were supposed to patrol the river and keep Sitting Bull's band from crossing so General Crook's forces and yours could close in on them."

"Hell, General, that's a laugh," Boyer cut in. "They could have crossed anytime they wanted to. In fact, big bands of them did, and they ran off our horses, or tried to."

"General Terry was afraid they might make for Canada if they knew we were all closing in on them," Custer said. "What do you think the chances are they might try to do that, Mitch?"

Boyer looked grim. "They ain't gonna run, General. The word's been out for over a year, by the moccasin telegraph, that Sitting Bull's been making big medicine, getting all the tribes to make war and run out the whites."

"Fat chance," Custer said.

I had to agree with that.

"You're going to have a big fight on your hands," Boyer advised.

"The Seventh can whip hell out of all the Indians we're apt to run across," Custer assured him.

Boyer just looked at Custer with an expression that said: "You'll be goddamned lucky if you do."

"What do you think, Bradley?" Custer asked.

"I'd guess we're going to have our hands full. There's a lot more of 'em than we thought. Boyer's right. It's a good thing General Gibbon didn't tackle them alone, although I didn't think so at first."

"Well, the Seventh isn't General Gibbon. You sound like you might think we can't handle them alone, either."

"I didn't mean to imply that, General," Bradley said. "But with all due respect, my opinion is there's no point to dividing our forces if Mitch is right. They won't run, and we couldn't stop them if they did. So why not hit them with everything we have?"

Custer said: "Infantry would only slow us down."

Boyer saw that Bradley was afraid to say what they both were thinking, so he said it for them: "If the Indians ain't running, and they won't, the infantry'll get there, too."

Custer laughed. "Indians always run from a superior force."

"We may not have one," Boyer said.

"We'll soon find out, won't we?" Custer was getting a little impatient with this persistent differing with his opinion. "I thank you gentlemen for coming."

Custer's cognac commentary:

"We might have pulled it off, Tom-Two. We just might have."

★ ★ ★ ★ ★

Brad and LeForge rose and shook hands with Custer again. He didn't stop me when I went out with them, but he called me back when I was a few steps away from the tent.

"Stay a while, Tom-Two. We've hardly had a chance to talk. I'll send for Tom-One and Bos. And you haven't met my nephew Autie Reed. He's about your age. Likes to fish, too."

We didn't know it then, but if Autie Reed was going to do any more fishing, he had to get it in during the next three days.

But we had a pleasant time jawing over old times, and the last thing Custer said to me was: "It looks like General Terry is planning to send you back to dancing school. If you can jump ship, come with us."

"I will. In fact, I'll stay right now if you can put me up somewhere."

"Easy. You can share Tom's dog tent."

I did, too. In a way I wish I hadn't.

Chapter Fifteen

The meeting on the *Far West* that resulted in Terry's order, that I've given you with the two word changes, is famous today among Custer nuts. Everyone who had been there, except Custer, has left his version of the meeting for posterity. Up till now. You read what Autie had to say about it, and I agree.

All of this is old stuff to Custer students—except for Custer's cognac comments—and there are a lot of them today, and they're a contentious bunch. That order is the symbolic bone of contention that they gnaw over and over. It's the centerpiece of the great Custer controversy, the question being: Did Custer disobey his orders? It follows that other implied questions are: And spoil the certain success of Terry's strategy which otherwise would have been achieved?—*as Terry alleged after the fact.* And as a result did Custer get himself and a lot of the 7th needlessly killed in the bargain?

Custer's cognac commentary:
"You know what I thought about that so-called order. The damn' thing was like a shopping list where your wife scribbles at the bottom . . . 'And anything else that strikes your eye.' Besides, I only took orders from the Almighty, and sometimes General Sheridan."

By now it should be obvious that until fate worked out the disastrous result of that order, it was only a set of guidelines hardly worth consulting.

Everyone who was there, in June 1876, knew that events as they unfolded would determine what was actually done. Brad's diary entry says that they all understood that Custer was free to do just about what he pleased, and all who knew him expected him to bust a gut to get to the Indians and hog the glory. This reflects the belief at all Army echelons that he certainly *would not* meet more Indians than the 7th could handle alone. Obviously a few civilians, like Boyer, didn't share that view, and even Brad had his reservations. So did I. By then I was getting to be a Crow.

If Terry had believed Custer wasn't strong enough alone, he certainly wouldn't have divided his command, particularly since he himself was with Gibbon's even smaller force. You can expand on that and add: If Sheridan had believed that any one of his columns alone couldn't handle all the Indians they'd meet, etc., and if Crook hadn't thought his command alone could handle all the Indians it would meet, etc. As it turned out, they couldn't.

General George Crook, just up the Rosebud a little over a week before Custer's fight, and largely through poor generalship, got his ass whipped by less than half the Indians Custer fought. He made the same mistake as Custer, dividing his command before he knew what he was actually facing. Fortunately for him, he had a lot of infantry firepower with him and it saved the day while he was reuniting his command. Infantry was stronger than cavalry in a stand-up fight because it didn't have to detail every fourth man to hold scared horses, which gave a fourth more men on the firing line. Green cavalry horses, of which there were a lot, always tried to break and run under fire, and, when they did run, they would carry away half a man's ammunition if he had been careless enough to keep it in his saddlebags. In addition, an infantryman had a rifle that would shoot a mile—and the Indians weren't anxious to close with them as a result. If Custer had had a half dozen infantry companies to rally on for reunion of the regiment, he'd have done a lot better. At the very least, his casualties wouldn't have been so much as half as high.

I will tell you the highlights of Custer's movements right up till I saw him killed. I will tell what I know for sure about what he ordered his subordinates to do. I know what he told them because I was at his side most of the time. The later cover-up stories vary a great deal from the facts as I know them. When those people who were covering up learned that I was alive and realized that the truth I carried around in my head could ruin them, my life was in danger every moment. They had thought that I was one of the missing who'd been killed and never found. You can imagine the dilemma that caused for Terry. As you'll see, he'd been led to make false reports by liars, principally Captain Frederick Benteen and Major Marcus Reno. Unlike them, he certainly would not have tried to seal my mouth in the manner they did, although, after I told him what I knew, he tried hard enough to seal my mouth. Even his sisters joined in that effort. But I'm getting way ahead of my story.

I was watching from a distance when Custer paraded the 7th for Terry about midday on the 22nd of June, as he pulled out on his last campaign. He had a little over three days to live. It was a nasty day, a cold wind from the north blowing low clouds across the sky. As a result, the horses had the wind up their butts and were hard to manage for the shivering troopers who were hoping to get the campaign over quickly, and cussing show-off officers. They wanted to get down the trail and root out their coats.

I took the precaution of being behind the little ridge overlooking the affair, so Terry wouldn't spot me and put me in irons. Custer led off, then rode on to join Terry, Gibbon, and a few others who were reviewing the parade. Almost everyone who's read much about it knows that as the 7th finally passed and Custer was shaking hands with all of them, Gibbon said half jokingly—"Now don't get greedy, Custer, and hog all the glory, save some for the rest of us."—and that Custer allegedly answered ambiguously by saying: "I won't."

Then he rode away to glory.

There was an old music-hall song in those days that went: "Forty miles a day on beans and hay in the regular Army-o. . . ." Forty miles wasn't considered excessive for a cavalry horse in good condition. After a month on the trail the horses of the 7th were hardened and in top shape. I mention this since much has been made of the allegation that Custer pushed the 7th by forced marches and exhausted his horses, which contributed to his eventual defeat. This misconception is based on outright, self-serving lies circulated by Benteen and Reno, and supported by Lieutenant Wallace, who was keeping the itinerary. (I never figured out why Wallace threw in with them; they must have had something on him.) In any case, this lie gave Terry the initial misinformation on which he based reports that were the opening salvo in the destruction of Custer's reputation. After Terry's reports got to Sheridan, Sherman, and Grant, Terry could hardly have confessed to being duped if he wanted to keep his reputation, especially since Grant loved to think that Custer had destroyed himself through rashness and deserved his fate.

Regarding pushing our horses, at the end of the first day we had only gone ten miles before Custer ordered a halt to camp. The next day we went a little over thirty—hardly wearing out our horses. Like I said, I always wonder what forced Wallace to go along with Benteen and lie about it.

I, for one, enjoyed the scenery, riding near Custer most of the time. Even he seemed to enjoy the country around us. He appreciated beauty in all things, had an irrepressible zest for savoring life to the fullest, but he was also busy keeping in touch with his scouts, who were commanded by Lieutenant Varnum. (As Varnum later told me, Custer almost worked him to death on our ride up the Rosebud—and I was there witnessing Custer at his professional best, constantly seeking for information.) He was following Terry's instructions to the letter up till the assumptions on which they were based were overthrown by events. He was particularly concerned about scouting to his left to make sure Indians weren't skedaddling around him, as Terry feared they might, and as he obviously did, too. Having had the spring to watch Indians allegedly skedaddling, I didn't share the fears of either of them that they were going to lose some Indians.

Crook, I understand, had the same fears until he was rudely disabused of them. He had met his come-uppance, as I have said, just over a week before, only a few miles up the Rosebud from where we had got to by June 24th. Pity we didn't get there when he was engaged. Together, we would have soundly thrashed them, but, if we had, we would have had to figure that those we had whipped might have gone back to their main camp, and then the tribes might have run north, running roughshod over Terry and Gibbon while we slogged along behind.

Even as things played out, the Indians undoubtedly would have attacked Terry, just as they had Crook, if they had discovered his approach sooner. In such a case, he'd have been in a real pickle. Why? Suppose Custer had "leather-headedly" followed his written guidelines to the letter and fogged off south on a wild-goose chase. He would have been completely out of supporting distance of Terry and Gibbon.

Can't you imagine what would have followed if Terry had been killed in such a fight while Custer had been blindly off on a wild-goose chase up the Rosebud, rather than exercising the "discretionary leeway" granted him by Terry's "order", and, more importantly, demanded by good judgment?

It was exactly this possibility—that he would get beyond supporting distance of Terry—that prompted Custer to follow the Indian trail we were about to run across on June 24th. It cut right over to where he knew Terry was heading. Custer realized by then that there were probably more Indians than Terry could handle alone. I am sure that if Custer had doggedly complied with what later events conveniently caused to be called his "orders", and had continued up the Rosebud, and Terry had been killed, or even severely defeated, those "orders" would have been seen in their *true* light as mere *suggestions,* and Custer would have been accused of failure to exercise good judgment. I think he would have been in jeopardy of being court-martialed, as Crook should have been for his lack of aggressiveness.

1945

I had no sooner finished writing this than I noticed a bourbon bottle on the sideboard being picked up, and a big slug disappearing. Even more interesting was watching a cigar rise from the humidor, go into my clipper, then rise to be nicely lit, followed by clouds of smoke issuing from it into the air.

"Becher ass!"

"Becher ass what?" I asked.

"Becher ass they'd have court-martialed me. And should have court-martialed Crook. "

He'd obviously picked up that vernacular from our G.I. visitors. It's nice to have visitors when you're old and lonely. Especially when they are the ultimate authority that can confirm your own tricky convictions.

I've got to tell you here about Sergeant O'Malley. He's out of the service now on what they call "points", a system of demobilization that's been in effect since it appears that we can afford to release some troops who've done their job, a selection based on a point system. He's had four years of tough fighting, and that's what counts. I now have Sergeant O'Malley on the payroll, an old cavalryman by the way. I needed a man of all work, and he's proven a godsend. He can even "buttle" as he calls it, which means act as a butler. But mostly he's good with the yard, supervising workmen. And he can do anything in the line of wiring and carpentry. He's also pretty good at rivaling Autie for the booze bottle when he needs inspiration, though he's more of an Irish whiskey man than a bourbon or cognac man. As cavalrymen, they have a lot in common. Unfortunately O'Malley can't hear Custer talking and thinks I'm a dotty old man talking to himself. I don't mind. He's a gem anyhow.

His first name is Terrence and he refers to himself at times as "Mrs. O'Malley's little *bhoy,* Terrence." And, true enough, he's not big—the ideal cavalryman at about five, six and not over 140 pounds.

I've discovered he's good at handling research for me in places like the Southwest Museum and Huntington Library. He's developed a real interest in my story, too. I wonder if he thinks I'm making it up. If he does, I don't blame him. Plenty will accuse me of cooking up the Western big windy to top them all. Well, maybe I am. It's fun and gives me something to live for a little longer.

One day O'Malley had been reading some of the stuff written by the Custer nuts about the part of the campaign my story is into right now, and he said: "I just read where Custer came out of the meeting on the *Far West,* looking a little downcast. I wonder what was sticking in his craw?"

I made a note to ask him as soon as I had a chance, and sure enough he showed up on schedule that same night—I can usually expect him about midnight.

I was snoozing in my chair, and he woke me up, stirring around in the cabinet for a new bottle.

I said: "Autie, you know O'Malley. He's got a question for you, and I sorta wondered about it myself." I told him what was on our minds.

"Hell," he said. "That ought to be easy for anyone to figure out. Read those 'orders' of mine. They were sending me off on a wild-goose chase to make sure I didn't 'hog the glory'. For all I knew, Grant might have told old Granny Terry to keep me out of anything that could give me some good publicity. After all, there was talk about me running for President if I won a big fight with the Indians and got a lot of good newspaper coverage."

"That makes sense," I agreed.

"Another thing was that I didn't think we'd done enough scouting yet to commit our forces, but Terry wanted to get home and have his sisters pat his little round noggin. I told him privately . . . 'If we're going in blind, why not give me overall command and you stay here like a department commander ought to.' "

"Did he get pissed off at the implied reflection on him and Gibbon? After all, Gibbon was a bird colonel and you were only a lite colonel." So I don't confuse someone, "lite" colonel is Army slang for lieutenant colonel.

"No, but I didn't give a damn if he did. He knew Sheridan had talked about putting me in overall command in my brevet rank of

182

major general. It wasn't unheard of. If I pulled it off, they might even have jumped me to brigadier general from lite colonel like they did old Granny Crook."

"How about running for President?"

"Not likely, but a one-eyed Chinaman could have beat Grant after the way he screwed up. Hayes did. Who the hell was Hayes? No one had ever heard of him."

"But Terry didn't buy it. Why?"

"He thought about it. He'd have liked to go home and eat his meals at a table. He never forgave me for getting in trouble with Grant and, as a result, sticking him with a field command. Anyhow, I ended up flogging along on a wild-goose chase until we ran across that big Indian trail. There was the chance I needed."

It took me back seventy years. I was right beside Custer when the scouts came in to tell him they'd run across the trail. It looked like all the Indians in creation had been milling around. We also found where they'd had their big sun dance.

Custer called a halt and sent for all his officers.

"This throws a different light on things," he told them. "We can't be more than thirty miles from all the Indians in creation. I'm going to try to stay out of sight over here somewhere, for a day, to give Terry time to come up, then go after them."

There wasn't a single objection to that.

O'Malley had been reading about this part of the march, too, and wondered: "A couple of Custer's officers said he looked downcast, and they thought he had a premonition of being killed. I wonder if he did."

I thought that might be a touchy subject to bring up with Autie on his next visit, but I'd always wondered the same thing myself.

183

* * * * *

I waited till I thought he'd be in a good mood, with a couple of belts in him and a good Havana lit up, before I brought up the premonition subject. He was quiet for quite a while, and I feared I'd touched on a forbidden subject.

Finally he said: "I had a dream. I had it the first time the night we pulled out up the Rosebud. In the dream I was in our quarters at Fort Lincoln, downstairs reading, sort of like in the Raven, 'pondering weak and weary', when I heard sobbing upstairs. It could only be Libbie. No one was staying with us except our maid, and she was asleep in her quarters behind the kitchen. So I went up the stairs as quietly as I could, and listened. It was coming from our bedroom where a lamp was burning low. Libbie used to leave a light on for me so I wouldn't stumble over something when I came up to bed. I slipped to the door and peeked in. "

He was quiet so long I thought maybe he wasn't going to tell the rest, but finally he went on.

"Libbie was in bed sobbing her heart out into her pillow. I went in and sat on the bed and put my hand on her shoulder, not wanting to startle her out of a nightmare and scare her. She turned and half rose and looked at me with those big brown eyes as though she'd never seen me.

" 'What's the matter?' I asked her.

"She looked at me a long while with the most tragic expression I'd ever seen. Finally she said . . . 'Autie has been killed. I knew he would be someday.'

"I woke up from my own dream and you can imagine how I felt. I had the same dream three nights in a row. I didn't make it to a fourth night."

The next day I told O'Malley what Autie'd said. "Jeezus," he blurted. "That ought to be enough to take the starch out of anyone."

Chapter Sixteen

Custer still needed a lot more information than he had about the Indians. The Crow scouts told him that there was a high lookout point on the divide between us and the Little Big Horn, called The Crow's Nest, from which they could see a long way and maybe find out if there was a big Indian village on the other side. Varnum took a few Crows, Mitch Boyer, and Charlie Reynolds with him to take a gander, and I went with them.

We got there about an hour before sunup and took a little snooze. When the sun was just coming up, we turned out, looked around, and found we could see a long way to the west.

"There's a helluva big village down there," Boyer said to Varnum. "Biggest I ever seen."

Varnum looked through his field glasses. "I don't see it."

Boyer exchanged disgusted looks with Reynolds. I guess I looked disgusted, too. I could make it out, maybe because I'd learned what to see from the Crows. It was especially easy to make out the immense horse herd. An Indian could not only see horses farther away than a white, but he could tell how many there were with his naked eye.

White-Man-Runs-Him looked at me and said: "Boy Killer"—which was the Indian name he'd hung on me— "plenty trouble down there." What he said next ought to get a laugh translated into G.I. lingo, since it was what amounted to: "We'd better haul ass out of here pretty quick."

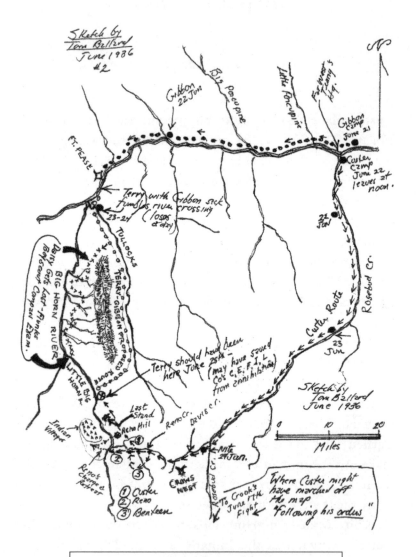

**Custer/Terry/Gibbon movements
June 21–27, 1876**

SKETCH MAP AND NOTES
BY TOM BALLARD

1.) Custer makes diversionary
    attack so his detachments
    can concentrate more easily

2.) Reno — who never received
    Custer's retreat and rejoin
    order

3.) Benteen — who fortunately
    disregarded his orders and
    was not far from pack train
    and Reno's fight

4.) McDougal bringing up packs
    that Custer urgently wanted

5.) Position Custer selected to
    concentrate both to shield
    Terry and perhaps join him

6.) Where Custer had hope to
    believe Terry might show up
    as early as the 25th in early
    afternoon. (He could have,
    but dawdled disastrously.)

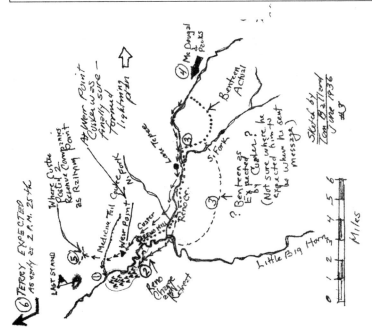

**Custer's 7th
June 25, 1876**

187

In the same terms, I said: "You won't get any argument out of me."

Varnum heard us and asked: "What did he say?"

I told him. He looked grim and said: "I guess I'd better send for Custer to come up, whether I can see anything or not."

(Before Varnum died, I had him down for a few days and we talked over old times. About the incident he said: "I couldn't see a damn' thing, but, with all of the rest of you telling me the biggest village in the world was there, I thought I'd better get Custer to look for himself. You were sure as hell right.")

We lay around up there waiting for Custer, and, after what I considered a long while, he finally showed up.

"Where?" he asked.

Boyer pointed. "Down there. It ain't as easy to see now, but you can see the big cloud of dust where the horses are, and that smoke is from a village. A damn' big village."

Custer focused his glasses and looked for a long while. Finally he said: "I can't make it out. Maybe I'm looking in the wrong place."

"Look down my rifle while I point it," Boyer told him.

Boyer held his rifle to one side so Custer could squint down the sights. After he was satisfied where to look, he scanned the area with his field glass for a long while.

"My eyes are as good as most, but I don't see anything but haze."

"Try to find what looks like a lot of worms crawling around. That'll be the horse herd."

He studied again, then shook his head. He was used to scouts getting cold feet when it came down to actually fighting their enemies in broad daylight. He said: "I think you men are having pipe dreams."

Boyer didn't conceal his disgust. I'm sure he shared LeForge's contempt for Custer and his kind of "experienced" Indian fighters.

Charlie Reynolds spoke up, which he rarely did uninvited, and this circumstance may have had more influence on Custer than anything that had happened up till then. Charlie said: "Best believe them, General. Those Indians are out there all right. Lots of 'em."

"How many?"

Charlie shrugged. Then, like Boyer, he said: "More than anyone ever saw in one place I'd guess."

Whatever the case, the real problem came right after we came off the hill. One of Captain Yates's sergeants had taken a detail back to recover a dropped pack, and they had run across some Indians rooting around in it. The Indians ran at the sight of the troops. From this, it was reasonable to assume that these Indians would report our concealed regiment to a village, if there was one nearby. As I recall, I read somewhere that they actually didn't. If they had, we wouldn't have "caught them napping" a few hours later as Custer put it.

I was watching Custer as he got this news, and he didn't look happy. He snapped: "Are you sure they saw the regiment? How close were they?"

The sergeant said: "They couldn't miss our tracks, all shod. They know we're here somewhere."

Custer angrily shook his head. "They could as easily figure we went on up the Rosebud."

Reynolds said: "In any case, they'll circle and follow the tracks. They know we're here, all right."

Custer really wanted to give Terry and Gibbon at least another day, and he was trying hard to convince himself we hadn't been seen so he could wait as he had planned.

Benteen was right there, and so was Reno by then.

As I said before, several of his officers have commented in memoirs that Custer had been unusually receptive to suggestions and actually asked for them on the march, an unaccustomed thing for him, and he asked them now: "What do you two think?"

Reno didn't surprise anyone by saying: "I don't know what to think. I know there must be a big village over there, somewhere, because we've seen the trail, and those Indians Yates's detail ran into will go back there and tell the others what they saw, sooner or later."

Custer looked at Benteen, who never tried to dodge a question. He said: "I doubt that their village is nearer than a hundred miles."

That was too much for Boyer, who chipped in: "And I'd bet a thousand dollars it's not over thirty. How about you, Reynolds?"

Reynolds nodded agreement.

Benteen, who had no use for civilian scouts anyhow, snapped at Boyer: "You got a thousand dollars?" His tone suggested he meant: "When did your kind ever have a thousand dollars?"

Boyer snapped right back: "Do you?"

Custer, who wasn't pleased with the way things had turned out anyhow, did his own snapping. "Let's cut the bickering, gentlemen! We can't afford wishful thinking." Here he'd finally faced reality and was talking to himself as well as to us. After a pause he said: "We're going to have to take the regiment over the ridge. Our name will be mud if the Indians run and we let them get away without a fight, and, if they attack us here, this is no place for cavalry."

Boyer, who had neither respect nor fear of big military reputations, put in his oar and said: "If I was you, General, I'd get us the hell out of here as quick as you can. There's more

Indians than you can handle."

I was surprised to see that, instead of blowing up, Custer actually smiled. "I think we can handle them," he said.

I thought: *Bullshit!*

1932

Regarding this episode, Varnum and I talked it out while he was on a long visit down to my place before he died. He didn't like to travel. Maybe he didn't have the money. Even retired colonels weren't rich. I had sent him a pass to travel on and had made it clear it didn't cost me a cent, because I was sure he wouldn't have accepted what might seem like charity otherwise.

He had phoned from the railroad station to let me know he was on the way out in a cab. He'd probably have gone back to Frisco if I asked him to wait for me to send down my chauffeur with the limo.

I was watching for him and met him in the portico. He got out and looked around before we shook hands.

"Some shed," he said, referring to what I always called "my place" in letters.

Then we shook, a good hard shake between old-timers who'd been the full route together and realized they weren't going to be around forever. He was a spry old bird for his age, and there wasn't anything dim upstairs, either. His eyes were still a clear blue and piercing. It's a pity he never polished the apples necessary to be a general because he was a real fighter.

I had Maggie fix some lunch for us, and afterward we went upstairs to my study. By then I'd started researching the Little Big Horn battle seriously and I got out my maps and spread them on the big library table.

Varnum said: "I never thought I'd be visiting you like this. In the old days I took you for one of Mitch Boyer's kind. Mostly Indian . . . judging from the way you could see just like them. I really couldn't see a damn' thing from the Crow's Nest. Couldn't see where the village was, and I'm sure Custer couldn't, either."

I nodded. "Here's where we were," I said, putting my finger on the Crow's Nest on the map.

"Custer was between a rock and a real hard place," Varnum said. "I wouldn't have wanted to be in his boots."

"What would you have done if you had been?" I prodded him.

"Let's sit down," he suggested. "My old cavalry legs aren't what they used to be."

I poured us both a big hooker of booze and we got comfortable in my big chairs. He was a bourbon man. I ran to single-malt Scotch for sippin' whiskey, which most had never heard of. At least Varnum hadn't when he asked me what the hell I was drinking and I told him.

He tossed down a slug of bourbon, let out a sigh, and looked at me directly when he said: "I've thought a lot about it, and I'd have done the same damned thing Custer did, using hindsight, and I'd have learned how from what Custer tried. On the other hand, if someone had turned over the command to me about then, I'd probably have shit my pants. But let's never forget that Custer almost pulled off the tactical coup of the century."

That didn't surprise me. I thought the same thing. Varnum was quiet so long after that, I thought maybe the booze had put him to sleep, but it hadn't. I prodded him a little again, and said: "Sergeant Slaper, who was in French's company, told me French said if he'd been in command, there wouldn't have been a fight."

Varnum snorted. "Hindsight. Let's think about that. Suppose Custer had holed up somewhere, maybe near water, back where Reno crossed the river. A thousand angels testifying would never have convinced Terry and the rest of the higher-ups he was justified in doing that. Every officer in the command, except Reno, would have made a stab at putting up some kind of fight before they knew for sure what a hornets' nest we'd kicked up. I read where Benteen said he suggested to Custer that he shouldn't divide the regiment with all those Indians around. I'm sure he never said it, or even thought it. Him, of all people."

I broke in: "I was right there when Benteen actually said he didn't think there was an Indian village within a hundred miles, but he didn't say it directly to Custer, although Custer heard it. Custer had to cut off Boyer who was making a fuss."

Varnum grimaced. "Good old Fred Benteen. You could always count on him . . . to lie, especially if it made Custer look bad. Let's just suppose that we'd holed up and the Indians pulled their freight, which they might have. By the way, where'd you hear from this Slaper that French said he wouldn't have fought? It doesn't sound like him."

"Slaper died here in the vet's hospital, out at Sawtelle. I saw him a time or two before he got soft in the head. I used to check up on him. He was in French's company, so he probably heard that, unless he made it up."

"Well, French of all people would have made some kind of fight. Let's suppose he'd been in command, instead of Custer, and hadn't put up a fight . . . he could have circled out of that creek valley we were in and gone north to try to meet up with Terry. We all knew Terry was supposed to come up Tullock's Creek."

I said: "I mentioned a thousand angels testifying, but it's

more likely that at least all the officers in the Seventh would have backed up Custer . . . or French as the case may have been . . . on taking up a defensive position or getting the hell out of there. If we had and the Indians had skedaddled after that, whoever was in command ran a good chance of being court-martialed for letting the Indians get away, judging from what I've seen of the Army way of thinking."

Varnum laughed, maybe to let me know I hadn't hurt his feelings. After all, he spent thirty-five years in the Army. "You're right there. Especially Custer, since Grant was already looking for a way to take off his head."

"You're mentioning Tullock's Creek brings up another thing they criticized Custer for . . . not sending that scout to Terry, down Tullock's, to let him know if there were any Indians around the head of it. What do you think about that? Remember him? A fellow named Herendeen."

"I remember him, all right. He was in Chicago at the Reno court of inquiry and he talked to me. He hated Reno's guts, probably because Herendeen himself was a real fighting man. He blew that story sky-high about Custer having fagged out our horses. You sound like you know something else about him I ought to."

"Not really, but I've read just about everything written about the battle," I said, "and they make a big thing of Custer not sending Herendeen to Terry. In fact, Major Brisbin and Gibbon later said that was because Custer didn't want them to find out what was going on and share the glory."

"Bullshit! Both of them hated Custer's guts. Pure jealousy."

"Why do you think Custer didn't send Herendeen?" I asked Varnum.

"By the time Herendeen was where he could get through that rough country between us and Tullock's, Terry himself would already have been halfway up it and could see for himself, or his scouts could have if they had been halfway competent. That brings up another point. Why do you suppose Terry cut off like a Boy Scout and got lost in the breaks over along the Big Horn when his own officers could have told him Tullock's was smooth as a billiard table? He got to us a day late and a dollar short as a result. He might have been where he could hear our fight on the first day, if he'd pushed right along without getting lost, and he could have come in and saved Custer and his five companies."

"I don't have the foggiest notion why Terry ever did anything, especially trying to send me to dancing school. Or why it's never come out in all the books that Terry was planning to come up by way of Tullock's."

I had to tell Varnum about cotillion, and he almost split a gut, just like everyone else I ever told.

It is extremely important, in any case, to know that Custer expected Terry to come by way of Tullock's, because that presumption shaped all of his actions after he actually located the Indian encampments and was finally sure of their immense size. This explains all of Custer's moves.

After dinner Varnum and I retreated to my study again for a little chemical libation and some more gab about the old days and the people we both knew, most now dead. He was the last surviving officer of the 7th that had been at the Little Big Horn.

The face of each of those other old-timers came back to me as we discussed them, and I could see them all around Custer at his last officers' call. As Custer's chief of scouts, Varnum wasn't there, as I recall. I asked him about that.

He said: "I got back down from the Crow's Nest and hunted up something to eat and some coffee. I'd been on the go for days and had missed a lot of meals. I was practically asleep on my feet, too. I always wondered what went on at that meeting."

"Well, I reckon I can tell you, since I was where I could hear everything Custer said."

"Shoot," he said. "I'm all ears."

It was a serious-faced group, for the most part. They were all gathered for the final time, none of those about to die suspecting their fate, except perhaps Custer. Of those present, the whole Custer contingent was going to be dead by sundown that night—Autie, brothers Tom and Boston, nephew Autie Reed, and Jim Calhoun, Custer's brother-in-law. All the officers and enlisted men of companies C, E, F, I, and L would be wiped out with them, with the exception of six men from each company about to be detailed to the pack train.

As usual Benteen looked surly and insolent. He didn't say a thing he later said he had in order to make Custer look simple-minded after he was dead and couldn't protect himself. As General Miles said: "It's easy to kick a dead lion."

Custer said: "We are going to have to go after those Indians or they'll come after us. I wanted to wait another day, but we can't afford to. After we get across the ridge, I intend to scout as much as possible to develop where the Indians actually are. According to the scouts, there are going to be enough of them to give us a good fight. I'm depending on each of you to keep your companies well in hand and get the best out of them."

He paused to see if anyone had a question. No one spoke up.

"OK," he said. "We'll move out in the order you report your companies ready. Whoever is ready first gets the lead, and whoever is ready last is the lucky one that minds the pack train."

He smiled. He knew no one wanted that bunch of balky mules that hadn't been trained to carry packs and the couple of dozen cussing packers who tried to manage them.

Benteen said: "My company is ready to move right now." It's doubtful that it was, but he'd seen enough of pack-train duty the first day out, not that he needed an excuse to lie. Later, true to his petty nature, he claimed that his immediate readiness somehow disconcerted Custer. (If it did, it was because Custer also doubted him.) In any case, I didn't think Custer looked disconcerted. Why should he? I still don't see what sort of honor is involved in taking the lead, but it beat hell out of taking the rear and eating dust. That turned out, soon enough, to be happy Tom McDougal, who was not too happy at his fate.

Custer turned to John Burkman and said—"I think I'll ride Vic today."—then he turned back and said to Reno and the company commanders: "Before you move out, detail six men and a non-com to report to whoever ends up with the pack train. I'm going to be right here until you all form up. Those six men are going to reinforce the company guarding the train, especially the reserve ammunition. We can't afford to lose that."

Being on those six-man details saved the lives of at least thirty men who would have died with Custer. After McDougal ended up with a thankless job, it actually turned out he would have a key rôle during the rest of the day. His sizable force heavily reinforced Benteen and Reno at a critical moment and was responsible for the fact that any of the 7th survived the battles of the 25th and 26th.

Custer rode up and down the lines after mounting up to see that the arrangements suited him, galloping Vic the full length of the strung out command. I rode right beside him on Buns.

He gave McDougal, at the tail end, some final words of encouragement, then returned, down the whole line, at a gallop to the front where his guidon bearer had been waiting.

I felt ready for a fight just watching Autie. I thought: *He's been in a lot of fights and isn't scared . . . why should I be?*

His face actually glowed in anticipation of battle. It shows what a good leader can accomplish by example, because, up till then, I wasn't anxious to see any Sioux—or Cheyennes, either.

He led the way up Davis Creek, crossed the divide, and proceeded down a tributary of the Little Big Horn that has since become known as Reno Creek. On our way down, Custer halted the column and assigned separate battalions to Reno and Benteen for reconnaissance to clear up his uncertainty about where the Indian villages were, their actual size, or even if there *were* any nearby.

I recall Benteen sitting his horse, receiving his orders, and as usual looking hostile. He wasn't as fat as he'd been when we set out, since the trail had taken some of the lard off of him, but he still had his fat, pink face and poppy-blue eyes. I think he had something wrong with him, maybe thyroid trouble. Later he said that, at the time when the regiment was divided, he had argued with Custer that we should keep the command together in view of our ignorance of the number of Indians. If he'd believed then that those Indians were around, he'd have acted a lot different a little later when he dawdled along after being ordered to hurry. In any event, I was right there and heard all that was said, and he certainly said nothing of the kind.

Custer told Benteen: "I want you to go out a few miles to the left and work down toward the river to make sure we don't have a bunch of villages all along it, like we found at the Washita. Then circle back and come in behind Reno, who will be on my left."

Benteen was probably glad of a chance to cut loose from under Custer's eye and said only: "Yes, sir."

I knew what I'd seen from the Crow's Nest, but I hadn't argued with Custer to try to convince him how many Indians we would be facing and that his scouts had told him exactly where they were, especially since Charlie Reynolds had spoken up, and if *he* couldn't convince Custer, nobody could. But somebody should have argued with him, just as Benteen claimed he had.

I thought sending Benteen off with only three companies was mighty risky, but at the time I wasn't worried about losing Benteen who, I thought, would have been a small loss. I see today that wasn't fair to a real fighter, and I remember what Custer told Libbie that day I overheard them in their quarters at Fort Lincoln: "I can't spare him, he fights." Benteen did, indeed, fight, and did more than anyone to save the remnant of the 7th after Custer was wiped out. It's a cinch Reno didn't.

Reno idly saluted to acknowledge his orders and didn't say anything. He and Custer seldom exchanged any words. They mutually detested one another, with most of the spleen on Reno's side, since he was jealous of Custer's reputation. Custer, for his part, knew that Reno had pulled strings all through the Civil War to be assigned to bulletproof jobs near his wealthy in-laws in Harrisburg, Pennsylvania. Despite that, but due to the family pull, he was awarded a brevet as brigadier general for his "distinguished" war service.

I'm hitting the high spots here, since all the underbrush that's grown up in writing simply obscures the main points because the writers are all speculating. *I am not speculating. I was there.*

After Benteen's battalion left, the balance of the regiment continued down Davis Creek and found the now renowned "burning teepee".

Custer rode up beside the tent, which hadn't yet been set on fire, and looked in through a gash cut by one of the Crow scouts. He looked at me and said: "Ever see a dead Indian? Sheridan claims they're the only good ones." He was grinning.

"As a matter of fact, I made one of my own."

He looked surprised. "You didn't tell me that."

I said—"The son-of-a-bitch tried to steal Buns."—and it was no time to explain the rest.

Inside were dead warriors on burial scaffolds. They were probably casualties from the earlier fight with Crook. Our scouts fired the teepee, but didn't go inside to scalp the dead, for a wonder. Undoubtedly superstition prevented that. There had been a small village on the spot, but, I think, our approach scared the Indians away in panic, since they left the bodies and a lot of camp equipment behind.

In case anyone believes all that bullshit about how charged up the troops were to fetch themselves an Indian, I had had a lot more experience by then with the Indians we were going to face, and would lots rather have been somewhere else, even cotillion. The average trooper was no different than me. Some of them weren't expert riders by a long shot and knew it, and many were bum shots because, as I said before, the Army never provided ammunition to practice with. They hadn't lost any "Injuns" and didn't want to find any.

My bung hole had begun to pucker as soon as we started down Reno Creek, since I knew the scouts were right about how many Indians we'd find—too damned many. I got another sight of the smoke from the village through a gap in the bluffs along the river, about ten miles off. Buns, who had a lot more sense than the average horse, or man come to think of it, must have sensed what we were headed into, and kept trying to turn around and take us back the way we had come.

A little farther along, Custer sent Reno's battalion to the other side of the creek, probably to hold down the dust we were raising. If the Indians hadn't spotted our dust cloud, they, indeed, had been "caught napping".

A word is in order here about why Indians were so often surprised despite their reputations for being wonderful scouts. Each Indian was his own man except in the camps where camp police were detailed to enforce order. But so far as obeying a chief who might have ordered a detachment out to scout, it simply didn't work that way, and anyone sage enough to become a chief wouldn't have thought of trying to give such an order. Indians fought as loners—each his own man. For this reason, such ridiculous rubbish as you'll find in Joseph Mills Hanson's book, *Conquest of the Missouri*, about how the downfall of the campaign of 1876 was due to an Indian military genius of the caliber of Stonewall Jackson is pure bosh. He was talking about Crazy Horse, which brings up another point. By the time Hanson wrote in 1906, Army propaganda had put the finishing touches on demoting Sitting Bull from the most respected Sioux chief to a cunning, cowardly medicine man. Let me assure you that Sitting Bull was the only Indian on the plains with the prestige to have got together a village of the size we were going to strike, and to keep it together for very long. He achieved that prestige from years as a warrior. As the Indians all said: "He was the Old Man Chief." Crazy Horse was a chief, but not of that stature, and he was also a notorious womanizer, which almost got him killed at least once. Being Old Man Chief didn't mean even Sitting Bull could give orders, though his advice would have carried great weight even with wild young warriors.

This should make it clear that we were about to pull a

boner in attacking that huge village that was the equivalent of kicking an ant hill. When we did it, warriors streamed out in clouds, all bent on attacking us. Unfortunately we ended up standing in that ant hill too damned long.

1945

Here I heard that familiar voice again. By this time, over the course of a few months, several cases of "the stuff" and several boxes of cigars had been devoted to O'Malley and the Midnight Imbiber. Bear in mind that I never actually saw the man behind that voice. But just here I heard him again.

"That's a fact," he said.

"What's a fact?"

"We stayed around too damn' long."

"Would you have done anything different if you had it to do over again?"

"Yeah. I'd have let Grant fire me and gone on the lecture circuit, then taken some of the high-paying job offers I was getting from robber barons. Second best, I should have simply obeyed those fabulous 'orders' that sent me off on a wild-goose chase up the Rosebud. Maybe I'd have run into Crook and we could have gone fishing together for the summer, like he did, and actually got away with it."

I laughed. "What do you suppose would have happened?"

"Terry and Granny would have had a hot time in the old town. Maybe they'd have got rubbed out. I might have ended up a scapegoat, anyhow, and taken one of those jobs with a robber baron after the dust settled. They didn't have any scruples against hiring a tricky devil . . . that's the kind they wanted."

So much for heroics.

June 25, 1876

Back to the ant hill.

One of our white scouts, Fred Girard, brought the news to Custer that started the fight. He yelled: "Here are your Indians, running like devils!"

He'd spotted a bunch of braves and thought they were running. Who they were and what they were doing is easy to figure if you know much about Indian tactics. They were the men from the small village where we'd found the teepee full of stiffs, and they were covering the flight of their women and children. They were also trying to lead us into a trap by having us pursue them to the huge village that was not far ahead. They were successful on both counts.

Custer ordered Reno to pursue the fleeing Indians and pitch into them. Custer would support him with the *whole* outfit. Don't forget the *whole* outfit included Benteen's battalion and the pack train. This implied waiting for them to close up, if possible. But Custer wasn't one to stand on one foot, waiting. He still wanted more information.

He'd been eyeing the high ground to our right all along. He turned that direction and yelled back to his adjutant, Cooke, known as Cookie: "Bring the rest after me! I'm going up there and take a look around!"

I was right beside him on Buns. As I said earlier, he was on Vic that day, a fast, high stepper, but Buns could keep up.

"We can see a lot better from up there"—he pointed ahead—"and still get right back to Reno if he gets in over his head."

I have no idea why he thought he ought to tell me that, but it was a fact. In any case he was right about being able to see a lot more country. Unfortunately we couldn't see enough of it soon enough.

When we hit the first rise, we could see Reno charging down a valley with retreating Indians running ahead of him.

Custer waved his hat in an encouraging gesture, and I later learned that some of Reno's troopers actually had seen him. Then Custer ordered the command into a slow lope and we cut out parallel to Reno's charge, but out of sight of it.

He pointed to a high hill ahead on our right and yelled to me: "I'm going to get up on that high point and look around! Tell Cookie to keep the troops down here, out of sight. You can come up if you want." Then he dug in and went up the hill that has become known as Weir Point.

I told Cooke what Custer had ordered, and then spurred after Autie and hit the top in a dead heat with him. Buns' big ass was built for uphill work, just like a bear's. When we got to the top, I discovered it was indeed possible to see all around, and what we saw must have puckered even Autie's doughty bunghole. It sure as hell ratcheted mine down another notch.

From Weir Point we could see the dense clumps of the tents of the collected tribes stretching for miles up and down the valley. If anyone thinks Custer entertained notions of attacking after that gander, they'd accuse him of being willing to attack hell with a squirt gun. Or Chicago with a regiment. He wasn't nuts. Far from it. (I hope I'm not hurting his reputation here. I suspect he always kinda liked to be considered nuts.) I'm surprised he didn't speak up about this later, some midnight, with the cognac working in him.

We came down off Weir Point, and Custer called his officers together for a quick meeting. There were five: Captain Myles Keogh, Tom Custer, Captain George Yates, Lieutenant James Calhoun, and Lieutenant Smith. "The scouts were right," he said in his quick, high-pitched voice. "There's more Indians over there than anybody ever saw. We've got our hands full. We've got to reunite the regiment as quick as we can and get in position to meet Terry, and keep those Indians from attacking him before we can cover him." Then: "Cookie, come 'ere!"

He dictated brief orders to Benteen and McDougal to bring up the packs and the reserve ammunition. After he dispatched couriers with the orders, he said: "We've got to get Reno to hell out of there, too."

I was surprised to hear him cuss, even under the circumstances, but the old Custer was coming out at the end.

"Why don't we go over and join Reno?" Captain Keogh suggested. "At least, we'll be near water while we're waiting for Terry."

Custer cut him off. "If we go down there, Terry may never get here."

A messenger was sent off to Reno, but he never got through. Nonetheless, Reno's chicken heart accomplished what Custer wanted, but not exactly the way he expected. Reno ran in a panic. So much so that Captain French confessed to having an almost uncontrollable urge to kill him for the poltroon he was.

Can you imagine how satisfied Reno would have been to use that message from Custer to get himself off the hook for not holding his position? He was blamed for Custer's death on account of running out of there and releasing a cloud of Indians to hit Custer. He was more responsible for killing the other two hundred, or so, that had been with Custer. A few years later I would have testified for him about that order if he hadn't screwed that up for himself royally. But I'm getting ahead of my story again.

Custer was keeping Vic in hand all this time, since, like the war horse he was, Vic sensed action and was dancing around, wanting to charge off somewhere. Custer sat him easily, hardly realizing what he was doing with the bit.

He quickly surveyed our surroundings and said: "We're going to find a good defensive position to hold and reunite the regiment. Terry will be coming up Tullock's, so we should fort up where we can shield him and be in a position to join him, or where he can join us, as soon as he shows up."

He posted Keogh with two companies on a commanding hill to our right with the order: "I want you to stay up there and hold as a rallying force. Watch for Reno and Benteen to be coming in with the pack train. I'm going to take three companies down and create a diversion to help Reno get out of his pickle and to keep Indians off Benteen and McDougal."

He sent the three company commanders, of those that were going with him, back to their waiting companies, and headed down the coulée, then circled and waited for them to line out and follow. He waved his hand urgently to hurry them. Time was now of the essence. He kept looking around to see that no Indians were swarming in on us, and waved once at Keogh who had rounded behind his last company.

That takes us back to where I started my story. Custer left two companies as a rallying point, and took three companies down to the ford where he was shot, intending at first to do no more than make a big racket, but he saw an opportunity to do more. About a hundred yards short of the ford he halted and called over his officers for a final confab. By then a few scattered shots were coming our way from across the river.

He said: "I've decided to try to go in and capture a few women and children. If we can get even a dozen, the chiefs will keep their tribes around to parlay and, better yet, won't attack us while we wait for Terry. It worked like a charm at the Washita. We might not have got out of there without having hostages."

That last-minute change of plans, so daring and so like him, was probably what got him killed. Who knows? He had been planning to cross the river anyhow for a brief sweep into the edge of the camp, then retreat and join Keogh on the hill where he'd wait for Reno and Benteen to come up, covering McDougal and the packs as they did.

His final attempt to re-concentrate the regiment could have accomplished everything the situation demanded. First, it would have conserved his vastly inferior force; second, hostages would have kept the Indians from moving away before Terry had time to arrive and observe their numbers for himself; last, hostages would have made negotiations with Sitting Bull possible. What Terry did after that was his own look-out, not Custer's. But Custer's luck ran out. He should have got a medal for the brilliant plan that he almost pulled off, rather than nomination for scapegoat. I think if Custer's luck hadn't run out at Medicine Tail Ford, he would have been entirely successful. And let's never forget that if that poltroon, Reno, had come to the rescue on Custer Hill like cavalry is supposed to, Custer and scores of men with him might not have died.

You know what happened after that. I told it all at the beginning of my story. After I saw Custer shot at the ford, I headed for the Crow country with the scouts and didn't come back for a couple of years. Terry knew where I was but dropped his attempts to own me. His sisters wrote to me though, especially Fanchon, who even sent me her picture and asked me to send her one of me. I worked again for Tom LeForge, and then went over to Helena and some of the other camps and made a damned good living surveying. It was when I read about the forthcoming Reno court of inquiry in the paper that I decided I had to come back. The bastard waited until the statute of limitations ran out, so that it was too late for the Army to court-martial him, and then asked for a whitewash. And I knew that Benteen was in with him up to his neck. It was more than I could stand and I got myself a ticket to St. Paul for a talk with Terry. It was time to tell him what I knew. Or, at least, I thought it was. It turned out not to be the sharpest decision I ever made and almost got me killed.

Chapter Seventeen

I headed back to talk to General Terry by way of Fort Lincoln. There were a number of people there I wanted to sound out before I tried to convince Terry he had been barking up the wrong tree ever since Custer was killed. I knew it wasn't going to be easy. If he publicly acknowledged his mistake, it would not only hurt his reputation, but make his superiors look foolish for believing his inaccurate reports. I thought he'd do it anyhow; he was as square a shooter as any officer, and not typical of the West Point mental cast that closed ranks as soon as any member of the old-boy set was threatened. I really expected justice to triumph. Remember I was only pushing twenty, though I'd experienced enough in some respects to be twice that age. Sad for my hopes, my experience hadn't been among fancy-pants schemers, but among straightforward doers in overalls.

My first big surprise was at department headquarters where I announced myself and expected the general to trot out and give me his usual hug. The clerk who guarded the inner sanctum, a new one I'd never seen, came out of Terry's office and said: "The general is tied up."

I expected him to say something more, but he didn't. So I said: "Didn't he say when he'd see me?"

"I got the notion he didn't want to see you," the clerk said.

I almost said: "That's a bunch of bullshit!" If I had, I'd have been dead wrong.

I went back to my hotel room and thought that one over. It

209

didn't take long to figure out that someone had wired him about the private investigation I'd been conducting, and the questions I'd been asking, and of whom. He was also walking on eggs, knowing what the forthcoming Reno court might reveal that would dirty his skirts. He probably was making sure that he was never called as a witness.

Well, I told myself, *if he wants to play that game, I guess I'll have to throw a little scare into him.*

I was no longer the innocent Tom Ballard that got run over by the general's buggy only six years before. Since then I'd met a few men who made the ground tremble when they walked or, at least, thought they did, as much or more than Terry. I knew they all put their pants on one leg at a time, just like me.

I went over to Terry's mansion and asked to see Fanchon, hoping she'd be home and not visiting back East or out shopping. Luck was with me, and she was home. My reception with her was a different matter.

The maid took me into the sitting room where Fanchon was crocheting. When she saw me, she dropped it, got up, and, after looking me over carefully, gave me a big hug.

"Tom, Tom, we missed you!"

I thought: *From what I saw, that "we" may be out of place. If the general misses me, it would be due to poor aim. I hope the son-of-a-bitch doesn't walk in about now and queer my game.*

She sent for tea—in my case, coffee—and some cookies. Then she looked me over again, no doubt impressed by my respectably tailored, new suit. Money does wonders for guttersnipes. She may even have been thinking of seating me at the regular dinner table soon. We never got that far, since I left town the next morning.

"You look wonderful, Tom," was one of the first things she said, then: "What brings you to town? I thought you were getting rich 'way out West." She laughed, but may have been serious.

"I came to tell the general something he should know, but he didn't seem anxious to see me."

"Oh, surely not. He talks about you all the time. You were almost like a son to him." She said that wistfully, as though she thought he needed a son. I doubted it. "Can you tell me what you're so anxious for him to learn?"

"I'd better tell somebody," I said. "There's been a great injustice done."

I told her the whole story in as few words as possible. When I first mentioned the name Custer, I thought she might ask me to get out, but she stayed the course and never interrupted me once. I thought she was going to break in a time or two when her mouth opened, but I figured out she was merely gasping. I can't say that I blame her.

When I was through, she said: "This is incredible! The general has been grossly deceived by some bad people if what you say is true." There was little doubt in my mind that she believed me. "I'll see that Alfred talks to you as soon as possible. He must have been terribly busy not to see you. Why don't you move up here to your old room? I've seen that it's been kept ready for you, in case you ever came back."

"I don't think I'd better move out of where I am for now," I told her. I didn't want to feel vulnerable of violating their hospitality when I talked bluntly to Alfred. "I've got a lot of calls to make on old friends and shopping to do," I said. I finally got away, satisfied with her promise that I'd get in to see Alfred first thing in the morning.

She was as good as her word, and it turned out to be one of the most eye-opening mornings I ever experienced.

"Well, Tom," Terry said affably. "Sorry I was tied up yesterday. Something Washington wanted, and they wanted it day before yesterday as usual."

"I understand, sir," I said. He hadn't asked me to sit down.

"Fanchon told me your story. It's fantastic."

"It also is true."

He had trouble looking me directly in the eyes, but finally managed. "I have no doubt of it. It makes complete sense. I was always uncomfortable with some of those glib excuses."

Were my ears deceiving me? His had been some of the glibbest, but I never saw a general yet—or any Army officer for that matter—that didn't know how to clear his skirts. They by no means have a monopoly on it, but it has to come with the territory in their cases.

"A great injustice has been done, obviously. The question is what can we do about it *now,* if anything?"

This didn't sound quite so promising.

He looked at me for an answer to that.

I said: "It looks to me like we should make a clean breast of it. It's the only honest thing to do."

That must have hit him in the gizzard, because he prided himself on being a man of honor, and honesty is the foundation of honor.

"How should we go about it?" he asked.

"I don't know. I thought you would."

"A lot of people will be hurt."

"Only those that deserve it."

Another blow to his gizzard?

"There are always innocent people who get hurt in a nasty affair like this. That's why they say 'let sleeping dogs lie'."

I thought it might be more accurate in this case to say that, if we dodged the issue, we'd be "letting lying dogs sleep"! To say nothing of forgetting the "honored dead", some of whose bleached bones were still scattered on the distant Little Big Horn.

As the saying has been since Pearl Harbor, Terry was working on a PYA strategy. In case anyone forgot, PYA means "protect your ass". Could I blame him? He was human like the rest of us. But I also remembered all of those happy Custers, and what had happened to them, and poor Libbie trying to resurrect her dead husband's reputation.

By contrast, Reno and Benteen were working like the devil at that moment to clear their skirts since the recent Custer biography by Frederick Whitaker had put them on the hot seat, and had actually led to Reno's requesting a court of inquiry. He'd also been in one drunken or disreputable scrape after another since the Little Big Horn and was under sentence to be dismissed from the service for his latest escapade, which amounted to window peeping while exposing himself, which is to say "conduct unbecoming an officer and a gentleman". The only allowable sentence for that was dismissal from the service. Was Terry protecting this poltroon? Hardly. He was protecting Terry.

Terry had almost choked when I told him Custer had been killed, or mortally wounded at the ford. That alone relieved Custer of the blame thrown at him for the debacle that had followed. As for Custer's tactics and the undeniable underlying reasoning—that everything he'd done had been to protect Terry's inferior force—that, too, couldn't be faulted or denied. Custer, fantastically brave and resourceful, had almost pulled off the tactical sensation of the century, as Varnum had said. The good General Terry was faced here with a confounding dilemma. He had emphatically said in writing that Custer had "disobeyed" his orders, but he, who had dictated those orders, and everyone who ever read them, knew Custer had "exercised *discretion*" as the orders allowed, and, not only that, it had been the only acceptable thing to do if the truth were faced.

Finally Terry said: "There are things you don't know about this affair."

I saw the standard ploy following: People in high places must be protected. The national good must be taken into account above personal considerations, etc., *ad nauseum.* He wanted to muzzle me.

I asked: "You don't think I should go to Chicago, then? Frederick Whitaker is expecting me." I'd sent him a letter.

"I think you'll find it a waste of your time, and you might actually be putting yourself in danger if what you say is true."

I knew that, but I thought I'd take the opening he'd given me to pin him down. "Danger from whom?" I asked. I had enough native shrewdness, young as I was, to wonder if he knew something I didn't.

He looked uncomfortable and dodged the question with: "I think you can figure that out as well as I can."

Here he was practically admitting that he wouldn't put it past Reno and Benteen to have me put out of the way, and the best he could recommend was that I stay out of their way. (Which, by the way, suited his own desires.) I knew what he was covering up. He'd been a gullible goose. Was there something beyond that? Probably no more than a desire not to embarrass the Army, which meant Sheridan and Sherman, and let's not forget that "sacred elder", Grant, who was still living and was the principal architect of Custer's ruin. Best not piss off big power. Had they already put out the word that they wanted the whitewash they got? What Terry said next was my first evidence of that.

"I'm going to give you a letter to General Sheridan. I'd like you to talk to him before you decide whether you should testify."

★ ★ ★ ★ ★

So I went to Chicago with that letter in my pocket, and no doubt there was a wire on the way to Sheridan, in cipher, telling him my story in detail.

As soon as my presence in Chicago became known, I was to have a "hot time in the old town" of Chicago, as the turn of the century song went, or more accurately a damned cold one.

Chapter Eighteen

I had found Chicago a dismal place in the winter on my first visit there. I've been back many times after that and I always found it depressing, even on sunny days. Only April and October are passable months.

Frederick Whitaker had arranged a room for me in a small hotel not too far from the Palmer House where the Army would hold the Reno court of inquiry. I took a hack to my hotel, since I had no idea where anything was in Chicago and it was a bitterly cold night. I turned in as soon as I got settled, tired out by a long, slow train trip from St. Paul during which heavy snow on the tracks had kept our progress to a creep. I could check in with Whitaker the next day.

I hit the pillow and was quickly asleep, not stirring until next morning when I was roused by the smell of cooking. The hotel had a restaurant. I thought: *I'm going to like it here if the food is any good.* It was, and the room was clean and quiet. What more could a young man ask? I wasn't destined to enjoy it for long in any case.

However, Whitaker wasn't to be my first stop. Terry wanted me to see Sheridan first. After breakfast I took a hack over to the Headquarters of the Division of the Missouri. Sheridan had been there since the Chicago fire and had himself fixed up like royalty. In the eight years since the fire, the whole town had been built into a city of brick, where before it had been a warren of sprawling wood buildings that had gone

216

up like tinder. The Army had done well for itself. As I said, generals lived like little gods. And Sheridan was the "he general" west of Washington, the head hog at the trough.

This time I was expected and didn't have to cool my heels waiting. Terry had said he'd wire ahead and get me in to see Sheridan for sure. Major George Forsyth, who I knew from the Black Hills expedition, escorted me in to the general. He glad-handed me like an old friend, to boot.

"Good to see you again, kid," Forsyth said. "Come on in." He left as soon as I was inside, not introducing me. I suppose Sheridan had told him to clear out as soon as I got inside.

Sheridan was startling to see for the first time. I'd seen photos of him from his Civil War days, but he'd put on a few pounds, like about forty. Somewhat like Tom Rosser. But it wasn't his dissipated look that startled me, but, rather, the feel of the man. I felt electricity bouncing from him as soon as he looked at me. He was small, compact despite his overweight, had a bullet head with close-clipped hair, a large, walrus mustache, and black, killer eyes. Here was the look of a bulldog that never released a grip unless killed. He wasn't the type to get killed. Too wary.

The overall impression that hit my mind was: *This fellow has been the route, has seen and heard it all, and isn't especially impressed with any of it.*

He didn't say anything for quite a while, just kept looking me over, perhaps to make me nervous. I was used to that. I thought: *Look away, old boy, the thing I like best about your type is that you don't look bulletproof to me.*

As a matter of fact, speaking of bulletproof, I had a pistol in my back pocket—a Colt .41 Thunderer. I was by then a Westerner and, furthermore, was expecting trouble from anywhere, in view of my mission. If Reno and Benteen and their backers didn't know about me yet, they probably would before the day was out. Anyhow, I was heeled. Reno was a yellow little prick, too scared even to have someone butcher his beef for him, but Benteen was the kind who might have me killed, or even do it himself. It's a wonder the Army didn't frisk people coming into Sheridan's office. Maybe they did if it was someone not known to them.

"Have a chair, young man," Sheridan invited, indicating one by his desk with a finger. His arms were unusually long, very noticeably long, and his hands large for his size. I'd have bet he was strong as a bull despite being little, like so many small, squat fellows are. I remember his voice was just an average voice for a man, not deep, not high like Custer's, but I'd heard he could yell like a scalded dog when he wanted to.

"General Terry wired and said you had some interesting things to tell. He gave me a general idea. I understand you knew Custer pretty well."

Something in the way he said Custer suggested that his favorite wild man still occupied a warm spot in his heart.

"I was sort of a member of the family for a while, I guess."

He nodded. So had he been a member of the Custer family, before he was married. The talk was he'd been sweet on Libbie from the time she joined Custer near the front in Sheridan's department, during the war, and that it hadn't hurt the Boy General's career. I saw nothing wrong with that. I was sweet on her, too. Almost every man who ever met her was, with the possible exception of Benteen.

"So tell me your story."

I had rehearsed where to start and what to say, but it all wanted to tumble out at once. I began: "In the first place, Custer didn't die like everyone thinks. I saw him shot, and it wasn't up on the hill like those paintings show."

Hearing that hit him right between the eyes.

"Where did he die?"

"He got shot down at the river, trying to cross. I don't know if he died there . . . I saw them carry him away on a horse. He wanted to go in and capture some hostages, then get up on the hill and dicker with the Indians."

"How do you happen to know this?"

"I was right beside him all the way down to the river. He sent me up on the hill to see if Reno was pulling out . . . but more likely he wanted to get me away from the shooting that was starting . . . I looked back and saw him shot off Vic and fall in the water."

I saw it all again and almost sobbed. I'd loved Autie like a big brother, almost like a father.

Terry obviously hadn't wired all of this information, and it hit Sheridan where he lived. He'd loved Custer, too. He knew Custer had made him as much as any one man ever did. He owed him a lot.

But the significant thing, I was about to find out, is that Sheridan's first loyalty was to the Army and its reputation. Like most West Pointers, regardless of how harshly it had treated them, it still had put its stamp on them and they were never again entirely free of The Corps.

"I'll be goddamned!" Sheridan said almost to himself. "That explains everything."

"Yes, it does, General."

"Why didn't you speak up before now?"

"What good would it have done? Nobody would have believed me any more than they believe the Crows who told the same story. Or will believe the Sioux or Cheyennes who were there, who'll tell the same story if they ever talk."

Sheridan was silent a long while. I'd really given him a big dose to think about.

"I believe you," he said. "I'd have believed you then. It didn't seem like Custer. I wondered if he'd lost his mind? It wasn't the Custer I knew." He seemed to be talking to himself more than to me. He asked the same question Terry had. "What can we do about it now?"

"Tell the truth," I said.

He was mulling that over, buying time to think.

"Tell me the whole story of what happened from the time you left the Yellowstone and headed up the Rosebud," he said.

He got out a map, that he'd no doubt brought in anticipation of my visit, and spread it out on his desk. "Come over here and show me where you were when these events that you're telling me about happened."

We crouched over the map together, and I told and showed him the whole thing. When I was through, he said a startling thing in my view. "You'd make a good engineering officer. That's as good a briefing as I've had in a long time. You remind me of Custer. He never failed me, collected more information in less time than anyone I had."

I hoped he wasn't going to make a West Point pitch, and was relieved that he didn't. He just shook his head and let out a long sigh.

Most of all, I was impressed by how he'd put me at ease and I liked him for that and also the sense of power that you could feel coming out of him from some deep well of self-confidence. It was easy to see why he'd made the record he had and held the job he did now. He was the right man in the right place. I liked him.

This brought us back to what to do. He said what Terry had said: "If, as you say, we should bring out the whole truth, it's going to ruin a lot of people."

"If it ruins Reno and Benteen, I'll be satisfied."

"But they aren't the only ones to think about. It goes all the way from Grant down. We were all misled. If the truth comes out, Terry and I ought to resign, at the least. Maybe Sherman, too. I understand you've been very close to the Terry family. Do you want to blight the rest of his life and make those nice sisters of his ashamed of him the rest of their days?"

That argument hit me in the groin. I've always been a softy where women are concerned, and Terry's sisters were all sweethearts when it came down to it. I wouldn't have hurt any of them for the world, especially Fanchon.

If Sheridan had pushed me, then and there, I'd have got on the next train out of town. Of course, we couldn't really do what we would have liked to: Bring back all those sacrificed dead to their families, especially Autie.

Instead he said: "I'm going to let your conscience be your guide, son."

In view of some of the things I knew he had done, and learned he'd done since then, I wonder if we had the same idea of what a conscience was.

He saw me to the door personally, shook my hand, and said: "Leave your local address with Sandy,"—meaning Forsyth—"and we might all have dinner some evening."

With my conscience primed, I looked up Whitaker. I found him at the Palmer House. Going there, rather than sending for him, was damned indiscreet. Almost the first two people I bumped into were Reno and Benteen, walking together across the lobby. Benteen spotted me just as I saw him, which was my bad luck, because, otherwise, I'd have turned around and kept out of his sight. I judged from his startled look that he hadn't yet been tipped off that I was still alive. That's rather amazing, but maybe not, since the people I'd talked to at Fort Lincoln had no love for him, and I'm sure neither Terry nor Sheridan had, even before they learned what I knew.

Benteen veered straight for me and put out his hand. "I thought you were dead," he said. "It's good to see you alive. You'll have to tell us where you've been since the Little Big Horn fight."

I thought: *You hypocritical shit! You're glad I'm alive in a pig's ass!*

Nonetheless, I didn't see any way out of at least telling them briefly where I'd been. "I went back to Montana with the Crows." I added: "If I'd been smart, I'd never have come down with Gibbon in the first place."

Benteen laughed. "If you were smart. Well, we live and learn."

Reno was watching silently, looking stunned, but he got the implication of Benteen's remark all right. Here was another chance for me to be smart. If I had been, I'd have said: "You're right. I'm pulling out on the next train."

"I suppose you're here to testify," Reno said.

I side-stepped that one. "I'm here to see a Mister Whitaker. He said I might not be called on to testify."

Reno looked slightly relieved, but he had to have known that, if I told what he fully knew I could, the prosecution would move heaven and earth to get my testimony in the record. And Benteen knew that, if Reno's boat sank, his would go with it.

"Do you know where Mister Whitaker is?" I asked them.

Benteen shrugged. "Probably around here somewhere." He turned and headed for the front door, with Reno tagging along. The latter turned and said: "Come on up and have a drink with us later."

They both knew damned good and well that Whitaker had a room at the Palmer House. He'd recently made a lot of money from his controversial Custer biography and came from a well-to-do family as well. He could afford to

222

stay in that rather grand heap.

I finally found him and was taken up to his room to talk. He sent for Lieutenant Lee who was the recorder of the board, which boiled down in Army procedure to a prosecutor. Whitaker had lunch brought in, and we spent the entire afternoon reviewing what I'd told both Terry and Sheridan.

Whitaker was pleased as could be. He kept saying: "You're going to be our star witness. You'll sink their ship."

He wasn't the only one that came to that conclusion, which I was to have confirmed before the day was over—or, maybe I should say, before the night was over.

I didn't have the heart to tell him that I had, indeed, decided to take the next train out of town. I caught it a little too late as it turned out. My whole adventure wound down within the next couple of hours.

I was walking back to my hotel, which I had figured out was only a couple of blocks from the Palmer House. I didn't hear the footsteps behind me. Snow sometimes crunches, but soft flakes had started to fall and they muffled the sound of footsteps. It was early dark, the street lamps were just being lit, and I was enjoying the brisk air and exercise outside of the smoky atmosphere of a hotel room, when the lights went out for me. I suppose that's the way dying is. I've been knocked out a time or two and know how that feels.

When I came around, I was inside a moving hack and my arms had been tied behind me and a gag tied tightly over my mouth. I looked around. Two men were inside with me, one on the seat next to me, and the other across the aisle on the facing seat. As we passed a street light, I recognized the face across from me, and it caused my heart to skip a beat or two, and then speed up. It was that son-of-a-bitch that had grabbed me at the start of the foot race a few years before when Benteen had all his money staked on his man. I didn't have to figure very hard to guess who the man next to me would turn out to be. It was Benteen's star runner.

When I stirred, he spoke up and said: "I see you're coming to."

I wondered where they were taking me. In a few minutes we were in an area of warehouses, and the hack turned into an alley between two of them. The fellow next to me jumped out and waited for the other to shift me out to him. I'd have liked to say—"I can walk, you bastards."—but all I could do was mumble. The one shoving me said: "Be quiet!"

They hustled me out and into a deep doorway. One knocked while the other went back and paid off the hack man. I'd bet the driver got a big tip, but, in a place like Chicago, his kind undoubtedly saw a lot of men get rolled. He wasn't about to send help to me.

It dawned on me that I wasn't coming back from this trip. Especially after they got me inside and put me in a wooden crate provided by whomever had opened the door.

But they didn't put the lid on and nail it down, and I wondered what the hell they were doing. My hands were sweating, cold as it was, and my heart was beating so hard it hurt my chest, which was aggravated because I was breathing hard. I tried to make my mind work but panic was fogging my ability to think, which fed on itself. Finally, a voice in me said: *Get a goddamned grip on yourself, Tom. You can't let these scums kill you! You can get out of this if you use your head. Where the hell is your fight?*

I found out what they aimed to do all too soon. They trundled me outside on some kind of cart. I figured the box was to keep possible prying eyes from seeing two men carrying another between them, which might have aroused suspicions.

All I could see was the dark sky above me, and the tops of the buildings adjoining the alley with snowflakes drifting down. It was an unreal scene, like the worst kind of nightmare.

After a short ride, they dumped over the box and I rolled out, only to be jerked roughly to my feet and taken under the arms by both men. Then I saw where we were—on the bank of the Chicago River, some fifteen feet above its dark, dirty waters. My panic returned at the sight of it. They were going to toss me in, trussed up, and I wouldn't be able to swim. Poe couldn't have created a grimmer atmosphere, with the scene dimly lit by reflections of distant lights where warehousemen were probably working late. The light snow falling etched haloes around the lights.

A shadow of hope arose in me when the sprinter said: "It won't do for you to look like you were tossed in tied up. Gotta look like a drunk that just fell in." He untied my hands, but warned me: "Old Ed here has you covered, so don't try anything."

For a fact, old Ed did have me covered, with what looked like my own .41. I was one who thoroughly respected the drop, and he had the drop on me for sure. Under those circumstances you tend to think: *What the hell have I got to lose? Getting shot might be better than drowning.* Then, looking over the man with the pistol, I thought: *If I get a chance, you might get a surprise.*

As soon as my hands were free, I rubbed my wrists to get some circulation going. I was braving up as my Indian friends put it—adrenaline was pumping, giving me desperate speed and strength.

As though sensing what I had in mind, the gunman snapped: "Stop that!"

I was planning on making my move as soon as my gag was loose. A lightning kick to the right place ought to take care of the .41, but I had an even better chance if they'd missed the Derringer in my vest pocket. I thought I could feel it there, but had to be sure. I rubbed my hand across the front of my coat as though I were still trying to get my circulation going. I was elated to find my hide-out still there, but scared as hell I might not be quick enough. I imagine the coolest gunman that ever lived has such thoughts before he moves. What I really wanted was to get my hands on the .41 in case the rotten son-of-a-bitch dropped it when I kicked him.

I made my move like lightning but, in the bad light, didn't quite hit his oysters. The gunman spun a little to one side and was bringing the .41 back to let me have it when I planted one in his brisket with the Derringer. I spun and let his buddy have the other barrel, and didn't miss either time. I picked up my .41 and was just figuring to stroll back up the alley, looking innocent, and down the street when I heard a police whistle. Shots weren't unusual in Chicago, but still they brought a beat cop. This one was whistling for a back-up from the next beat, I figured. I saw the cop hit the head of the alley and stop, looking our way. I didn't know if he could make us out or not, but I knew damned well I didn't want to be on the carpet for killing a couple of soldiers.

I scanned the area for a nearby rowboat, and was disappointed. I could see no sure way of escaping down the docks and, besides, had no idea but what another cop or two might show up and cut me off. The river didn't look too inviting, but I'd been in water just as cold in St. Paul as a kid and just that spring, with Buns, had swam over the Yellowstone with ice still floating in it.

I thought—*What the hell!*—and leaped. I thanked my luck in having bought a fancy pair of side-gore shoes that I could slip off easily, and managed to get them off first thing when I was in the water. Nothing drags you down in water quicker than boots full of water.

By the time the cop or cops got there, I'd be halfway across. Unless they were crack shots, I wasn't apt to stop lead. But no one shot at me. Maybe I was hard to see among the floating packing cases and trash, and maybe, since my abductors hadn't been in uniforms, they thought it was just a gang killing and a favor had been done the city.

My main problem was that my wool clothes got heavier and heavier and almost sank me. I reached the other side, panting heavily, and grabbed a brace between two piles and took a rest. I saw lanterns sprouting on the bank I'd left and knew I'd better find a way to crawl out of there before someone came across the nearest bridge, or found a rowboat. My luck held and I made out a ladder a short ways down from where I was catching my breath.

After I made my way clear of the area, I debated going back to my hotel, but finally nixed that idea. They might be watching that, too. I knew who *they* would be. Some others of Benteen's company of hardcases, the same crew that floated a petition to get both him and Reno promoted after they'd sunk Custer's boat. I checked and found my money belt still around me and figured I could buy my way quietly out of this part of the country. My first stop was a Jew's second-hand store, open late to take in extra bucks. The owner, an old man who'd probably seen it all twice, had no comment on my condition and didn't even look surprised. He fixed me up with dry clothes, socks, and shoes, and I headed for the train station.

I saw General Sheridan once more, after he got his fourth star and moved to Washington, D.C. to take Sherman's job once he retired. I was with my new boss, empire builder Jim Hill. The Army owed him a lot for favors granted free, and

Hill owed the Army for the same thing. They scratched each other's backs, which was why we were in Washington.

Sheridan recognized me at once and seemed glad to see me again. After Hill and Sheridan talked and we were leaving, Sheridan said to Hill: "I'd like to have a word with your assistant."

Hill went outside and waited. He must have been curious, but, to show you what sort he was, he never asked me after I came out what we had talked about. I'm glad he didn't.

Sheridan said: "I never got a chance to tell you what I thought really ought to be done to Reno and Benteen."

I was all ears. But Sheridan remained quiet for so long, I thought he'd changed his mind, and finally asked: "What?"

"The bastards *should* have been shot. You and I both know that. But there are some things we can't do, regardless."

I thought: *I'll bet that's as close as he ever came in his whole life to an apology.*

I noticed there was only one picture on Sheridan's office wall. A huge one of Autie, by Mathew Brady, in which he's standing boldly in high cavalry boots, arms folded across his chest, wearing his gaudy, self-designed uniform, one leg thrown forward defiantly, and the fire of battle in his eyes.

Epilogue

After my escapade with the Chicago River and Benteen's plug uglies, I went back to St. Paul, first class, on a sleeper. I had put a little extra cash aside and decided to live a little. I liked the comforts of civilization and wasn't sure I wanted to stick to the frontier forever. I could send for Buns, if I found a proposition back in the civilized world. Little did I know.

The job I found was to keep me out of civilization as much as in for most of the next fifty years.

It all started when I was walking down the street the morning after I got to St. Paul. I was startled by the crash of breaking glass in an office building I'd just passed, and even more startled when I whirled around to see that it had been caused by a body being issued out on the sidewalk through the window. It wasn't a saloon, or I wouldn't have been especially surprised. The young fellow who'd crashed out the window picked himself up, apparently with nothing broken, and brushed the glass shards off of himself. I might have tried to help him except a burly man with a fierce black beard and glowering, ruddy face shot out the door just then. He shook his fist and his whole attitude suggested how the young fellow had been propelled out the window—he'd damned well been thrown. The newcomer yelled: "And don't come back around here ever, you stupid son-of-a-bitch!"

That set the young fellow off at a trot. He'd seen all he wanted of the fierce-looking, bearded fellow. However, once far enough away to outrun him if need be, he yelled back: "Fuck you, you old fart!"

I probably shouldn't have, but I laughed. I was a little surprised to see the bearded man laugh as well. He looked me over then and, obviously still irritated, said to no one in particular: "The dumb son-of-a-bitch!" He turned to go back in the building, but a new idea grabbed him and he turned toward me and asked: "How would you like a job?"

Naturally I was surprised, but not too surprised to ask: "What kind of a job?"

"A job. Anybody could beat that dunderhead at anything. He was keeping records for me. What can you do?"

"I'm a surveyor. Maybe even a jackleg engineer."

"Well, that isn't what he did, but it's something else I need. Do you want a job or not?"

"Sure," I said. "Try me out."

Like I said, I was a great believer in conserving my bankroll and always wanted to do something even while I was looking for something better.

And that's how I went to work for Jim Hill, the empire builder. I stuck with him till he died, and afterward stuck with the Great Northern for a total of fifty years until I retired. He made me rich. It was a two-way street, though. I helped him get a lot richer than he was when I met him, and he knew it and never denied it. Irascible he may have been, but he was a great boss and dead honest. He made no bones about his likes and hates. He once offered me a million dollars to shoot Teddy Roosevelt when he was President. The million sounded pretty good, but the idea of life in the pen or a rope around my neck didn't appeal to me. I talked Hill out of it without getting fired.

My courtesy call on General Terry was epic, too. He

didn't stall about asking me into his office this time. He waited for me to say something. I was certain he knew by then that two of Benteen's troopers had been mysteriously killed in Chicago. Although I heard the police were completely baffled, I'd bet Benteen wasn't. It's not likely that Terry was, either. I read the newborn respect in Terry's expression. He was facing a killer. He knew I had killed an Indian, but this was something different. More like Wild Bill.

I said: "I thought it over, after talking to you and General Sheridan, and decided the good of the country would best be served if I stepped out of the picture."

That naturally brightened his face.

There was more to our talk than that, and I saw the Terrys whenever I was in St. Paul over the next few years, until the general was promoted and went East. They were all very kind to me, and my friendship with them didn't hurt my new career at all. I'm being funny, of course. It helped the hell out of it, as you must suspect.

I did run into Benteen one time after that Chicago affair. He was coming up the street in Salt Lake City. By then he was a major. I saw him first and wanted to get close to him and yell—"Boo!"—but he spotted me, did a double-take to make sure who I was, and quickly turned into a store. He had that Wild Bill notion about me, too, I suppose. When I followed inside the store, he was nowhere in sight. He probably thought I might shoot him and so must have run out the back door. If I'd caught him alone out in the sagebrush, I sure as hell would have shot him.

1945

Christmas Season

World War II ended with the surrender of Japan in August. Our G.I.s were coming home and looking forward to it, in most cases. Some, like my newly acquired "butler", Sergeant O'Malley, didn't have homes any more. Those kind were staying in for a few more years to get their feet on the ground, or, like O'Malley, who'd been a lifer, retiring after thirty years of it.

O'Malley has never had a home he could remember, and seems happy with his home here, which I'm sure he is. I pay him a top salary, and he can eat and drink his fill on the house, has his own room, and the run of the place. He loves Maggie's nephews and nieces—and get this—they're teaching him to swim.

We've got a big Christmas tree set up, and Maggie is going to bring all the kids over in the morning to open presents. The lights on the tree are lit and a fire is going in the fireplace. It's been a chilly Los Angeles week like you get occasionally in the winter, and the warmth radiating into the room from the fire here in my study feels first-rate to old bones. I keep my chair shoved right up close in front of it.

I must have been dozing again and woke up to see a by-now-familiar ritual in progress by the liquor sideboard. A big hooker went down, then the cigar-lighting routine followed, another hooker was poured, this time a water glass full, and the two visible signs of my visitor came across the room in a cloud of cigar smoke. Something solid but invisible flopped into the matching chair next to mine.

"Ah, Christmas," he said. "Nothing like Christmas. I re-

member how it was when I was a kid."

"And . . . ?"

"Mostly cold," he said, and took another big slug. "Have you finished that goddamn' fairy tale you're writing?"

"Almost. I have to ask a personal question, and I don't want you to get mad."

"Shoot."

"Were you killed when you got shot at the ford?"

I saw the seat of the chair move as though he'd got up. I thought I'd pissed him off and he was leaving.

"Don't go," I said. "I didn't mean to pry."

"I'm not going. I'm gonna fill this glass again . . . 'tis the season to be jolly. I'm going to hang one on."

I watched as the glass was drained and carried across the room to be refilled. Then it moved back toward the chair.

"I've seen lots of guys survive worse wounds than the one I got at the ford. It just knocked me off Vic into the drink. They fished me out, and Tom hustled me onto a horse and I was even able to help a little. He held me up till we got up on the ridge. I kept wanting to get the companies together, but I didn't have strength enough to make a sound and that really pissed me off.

"As you know it finally all came unglued. I was in and out of it, but weak as hell and hurting too bad to talk. Tom found me a comfortable spot between two dead horses. Finally the fighting got down to just a few of us. You know that business about saving the last bullet for yourself."

"You shot yourself?"

"No. I was too damned weak. Tom shot me. That's where that hole in my head came from. Then a little later he finally got killed himself. You'll never guess what he did after he shot me."

He was quiet a long while. Finally he said: "He lifted me up and kissed me, crying like a baby while he did it, and said . . . 'For Ma.' Then he dropped me like a sack of potatoes and went after the

Indians with a pistol in each hand, yelling like a madman. You know Tom. . . . He practically screamed . . . 'You sonsabitches, you made me kill a better warrior than you stinking bastards will ever be!' "

That settled the only question that had still been in my mind.

We tied on a pretty good Christmas Eve buzz. After a while Autie said: "I wish Tom was here."

I said: "Maybe he is, who knows?"

"I do," he said. "He's down in Florida on the beach. At Key West. He likes to ogle the ladies in swimming suits."

I thought: Who doesn't?

He left then. It was his last visit to me.

I almost forgot I said I'd tell you, when I started writing this, what I was doing back there at the Little Big Horn in 1926, circling in that old Jennie. I'd promised Libbie Custer that I'd drop a wreath where Autie had been killed, and I did.

Well, Autie left, and it was still Christmas Eve with time for me to indulge my favorite pastime and saw a little more wood in my big chair. Autie was feeling no pain when he left and neither was I. I thought: *Maybe he went to join Tom on the beach at Key West.*

Something roused me again. The fire had burned low and I was thinking of going to bed. I wondered what woke me this time. I knew something was in the room with me and hoped that Autie had come back for another snort, hoped, if he had, that he'd brought Tom this time. I wanted to show Tom a photo of Buns' grave with its life-size bronze of him standing on top, looking suitably wicked with his gaze fixed off toward the Big Horn Mountains for eternity. I'd had Charlie Russell make it for me. Below on a bronze plaque fixed to the granite pedestal was my tribute to the best horse that ever owned me:

BUNS
Where is my boy?
I think I know.
In the great green pasture,
Where horses go.

Tom would have liked that.

But the noise that woke me up wasn't Autie and Tom. It was better even than that.

I smelled a familiar cologne and felt a warm kiss on my forehead and heard a woman's voice that I'd once known very well, indeed, from the long ago say softly: "Thank you, Tom-Two."

About the Author

Glenn G. Boyer, a Wisconsin native, left his home state for WWII and spent twenty-two years in the U.S. Air Force. He retired in 1965 as a command pilot with the rank of lieutenant colonel. He is best known worldwide as the foremost Wyatt Earp researcher and author due to his many publications on the subject, which were enlightened by his lifelong friendship with Wyatt Earp's family. With *The Guns of Morgette* (1982) Boyer started writing Western novels. This series, which now numbers six, chronicles the adventures of legendary lawman, Dolf Morgette. In *Dorn* (1986) Boyer sends up every cliché and stereotype of both the pulp Western genre and "B" Western movies. His historical novel, *Winchester Affidavit* (1997), is a tale of the classical cycle of Westerns sagas—from pioneer settlement of a locale, through the invasion of foreign capital that often led to violence in attempts to dispossess small settlers, through Hollywood's final distortion of the stories that regrettably has been accepted all too often as history. His fiction, deemed by *Midwest Review* as reminiscent of Zane Grey, Max Brand, and Louis L'Amour, is as notable for its sharp and penetrating characters and grippingly suspenseful plots as for the authenticity and accuracy of the historical backgrounds and settings. His next **Five Star Western** will be *Morgette on the Golden Strand*.